The Legend of the Lowcountry Liar

The Legend of the Lowcountry Liar

and Other Tales of a Tall Order

Brian McCréight

For Zoë & Aidan
to read with fun!
yours in the Telling,
Brian McCréight

Pineapple Press, Inc.
Sarasota, Florida

TO TERRIE,

WHO'S HEARD IT ALL BEFORE

Pineapple Press, Inc.
P.O. Box 3889
Sarasota, Florida 34230

www.pineapplepress.com

Library of Congress Cataloging-in-Publication Data

McCréight, Brian, 1955-
   The legend of the Lowcountry Liar and other tales of a tall order / by Brian McCréight.— 1st ed.
       p. cm.
   "A collection of folktales adapted to the South Carolina Lowcountry ... all related by narrator Jim Aisle"—ECIP data view.
   ISBN-13: 978-1-56164-337-0 (pbk. : alk. paper)
   ISBN-10: 1-56164-337-8 (pbk. : alk. paper)
   1. Tall tales—South Carolina. 2. Folklore—South Carolina. I. Title.
   GR110.S6M33 2005
   398.2'09757—dc22

                                                                2005013793

First Edition
10 9 8 7 6 5 4 3 2 1

Printed in the United States of America

Contents

Introduction

The first time I met Jim Aisle, he was casting a net for shrimp and crab on a sultry summer evening down on the Ashley River side of the Battery, the original seawall of Charleston. He was affable, generous with his hilarious stories, and perfectly at ease talking to a stranger while shrimping at sunset. He spoke of "epic fights and epiphytes," and I knew I had to hear more from this special Southern storyteller. I hope that you, too, will want to listen to the sounds of these stories as you read them. Perhaps you should read them aloud, and to others, in order to share a semblance of what it is like to hear Jim embellish a narrative.

Then again, you just might meet Jim someday, in downtown Charleston, or out at one of the barrier island beaches, or at least see him sailing by on his sloop, the *Coota*. If you have the time, ask him to tell you a story. He'll either lie or tell you the truth, but you'll have to determine which is which.

I still don't know.

~ *Brian McCréight*
Charleston, SC

The Legend of the Lowcountry Liar

My storyteller friend, Jim Aisle, is proud to be known as the Lowcountry Liar, and I had to know how he got that name—I already knew why.

Well-suh, I live down here 'round Chawl-stin, South Carolina, in the heart of the Lowcountry, the so-called Netherlands of the South. I am frequently referred to by the other inhabitants of these environs as the Lowcountry Liar. My name is Jim Aisle. That's a handle of Huguenot heritage, if you hazard to surmise. I grew up a Lowcountry lad along the Carolina coast among the barrier islands 'round Chawl-stin. This is the story of how I come to tell stories.

On any given day I might sail my sloop, christened the *Coota*, anywhere from the Edisto estuaries to the Isle of Palms archipelago. Often enough I would slip into the peninsula city to visit the age-old market, where among sundry Southern charms I could witness the Gullah women artisans weavin' wonderful sweetgrass baskets. I would watch 'em awhile, occasionally slippin' a few strands through my hands, plaitin' wisps of palmetto leaf or pine straw.

One slow afternoon I was down to the market, and I overheard the Gullah women while they was weavin' say that they likely wasn't a single, solitary reed of sweet sweetgrass in the whole Lowcountry that collectively they had not gathered, woven into baskets and such, sold, and already had the money spent, after expenses. The weavin' women also 'lowed how, despite the sometimes-sparse natural resources of sweetgrass or palmetto leaf, not a one of 'em ever collected nothin' from a certain, somewhat sacred, spot. The women spoke of a special someplace, where the shore and the sand and the swamp share the sunshine—a place south of the city, along the Stono Ribbah, known as Buzzard's Roost Point.

I knew enough to know where that location was, 'cause it be the very tip of the northeast corner of Johns Island. That a put it facin' West Ashley on the north bank and James Island on the east bank of the same elbow-bent ribbah. Why, early on a mornin' I could easily sail the *Coota* down Wappoo Creek where it cuts to the Stono, land at the point, investigate the flora, maybe take some of it for my own covetous collection. Who would know?

While I was deep in thought a-cultivatin' my plans, already rapt with my success, I didn't clearly overhear the reason for the agricultural abstinence. The women spoke softly, sometimes slurrin' they speech anyway, as if to avoid a curse, but they all agreed solemnly that Buzzard's Roost Point was an exclusive garden reserved for selective root doctors. These root doctors, or conjure men, would come to the point freely to gather necessary ingredients for one kind of mojo or another, and it was best for mere mortals not to trouble Trouble. Thus and so, all the basket weavers left well enough alone. Besides, with a name like Buzzard's Roost Point, alone was as it should be.

Well, the rest of the afternoon I hurriedly went about my secret business: first inspectin' the decks, refurlin' sails, tightenin' shroud lines; next, preparin' the assembled tools for the raid. I sharpened a hand sickle, although in my haste I erred from the weavers, who never cut, but always pulled the sweetgrass out by the roots. I oiled the blade anyway, and wrapped it in a croker sack. I tied loop knots in lanyards to lash the soon-to-be-gathered grass into bundles, and put 'em in another sack. I filled a red kerosene lamp, checked the wick. Then I fried some fresh fish for supper, ate some, and packed a lunch of it for the next day. Finally, I went to bed.

· · ·

Long before the rooster crowed, I had already slipped the *Coota* through the Wappoo Cut, anchored in the Stono, and rowed ashore to Buzzard's Roost Point. I was evermore inspectin' the plants of the place, havin' to feel as much as see, even with the lamplight from a wick a half-inch high. Wan light from a gibbous moon filtered down through shiftin' blankets of clouds slidin' overhead in silent darkness.

'Round a copse of crepe myrtle trees I finally found plenty of healthy sweetgrass, and with a glad sigh I set down my gear. It was time now to separate the reeds from the weeds. Time now to cut the bonds that tie to earth.

So I unsheathe the sickle and begin a-swingin' away with determination and delight. In no time, satisfied with my exercise, I bind up two ample bundles of grass end-to-end and stuff 'em into the sacks. Now, I ought to get off Buzzard's Roost Point before day-clean, as the Gullah folks call the new day's light.

As I stand up I realize the mornin' fog ain't yet lifted, and, tired from my toils up to this time, I decide to rest a spell. Besides, a hunger's been comin' on as the mornin's moved along, and the fog seems to be gettin' thicker, so, I unpack a fish sandwich and have lunch for breakfast.

With every bite it seems the fog increases. By the last swallow I can't hardly see my fingers outstretched before me. I stand up warily to survey the scene, but any known landmarks are invisible. A compass be useless.

Except, there—over there . . . to the west? A faint light of some sorts a-glowin'. Well, where they's a light, they's sure to be people, so I make for that vague light. I go empty-handed and absent-minded, without a thought for grass, sack, or lamp.

I'm in a fog in the fog, and if I trip once it's a dozen times, almost as if I'm gettin' grabbed at the ankles. Nonetheless, I endure the crashin' and bashin', and come upon a humble marsh-cabin set upon a rise of ground overlookin' the ribbah. The door's wide open and light from within pours out like a beacon in the fog.

I peer 'round the door to see a thin, wrinkled, black man with snow-white hair, and a very round black woman, maybe the wife, a-sittin' quietly in cane-back chairs before the hearth fire. The old man's suspenders be all tangled 'round he waist, he shirt and trousers appear as wrinkled as he skin. The missus wears a faded duster of pink and yellow flowers, her scalp be all covered with a dark blue bandana. Ain't neither of 'em wearin' shoes.

Before I can clear my throat to speak, they both turn, hail me a greetin', and invite me in. Well-suh, inside by a warm fire would surely be a reprieve from the clammy, unlit mornin', and these old folks at home seem to be expectin' company. So, I walks in and make myself comfortable on a stool they set between 'em. We pass some pleasantries as manners demand, but then they ask me how I happen to be in the neighborhood, and I realize that I cannot reveal the reason for my visit.

"I thought I might get some early, early fishin' done," I tell 'em. "Y'know, before it gets too doggone hot."

"You already catch the early bird's worm?" the old man asks with a grin.

"Yesss," I reply uncertainly.

"Hmph! I don't believe it," snaps the old woman. She pulls out a corncob pipe from a duster pocket, then a small tobacco pouch.

"Yes, ma'am. I mean, no, no ma'am. I mean, I ain't caught nothin' yet."

"Not yet?" the old man frowns.

"No, sir, not yet. I just got here, y'see, and—"

"See there?" the old woman asks, more like demands, noddin' toward a wooden pail. "Since you ain't done no woik and ain't caught nothin' yet, how 'bout you fetch a fresh pail a wata for me from the cistern?"

I hesitate a moment before speakin', which was better than tellin' the truth. "Uh, yes, ma'am, only too happy to oblige. Umm, where is the cistern?"

"Just off to the side, on your right," she says without lookin' up, steadily stuffin' strands of tobacco into the pipe. The old man nods at me like it's all right.

Outside again, pail in hand, I stumble over to the cistern. I fumble open the hasped half lid, feel 'round for the rope, and connect it to lower the pail. After haulin' up the full, heavy pail, I set it on the ground to level off, then reach over to close the lid.

Suddenly the wind kicks up, pullin' at my shoulders, and begins to lift me off the ground. Without a sound, I rise in a corkscrew up into the dew-wet, quilt-thick clouds. I may have passed over the Stono Ribbah, or I may have flown over Folly Beach for all I can tell, but then I rudely hit land—*bam!* I stop spinnin', or at least I think I have—I ain't sure.

Anyway, they's not light enough to see the tip of my nose. I think I hear, away in the distance, a low song—a moanin' chant. Sounds like some group a-singin': *"Swing low, sweet chariot, comin' fo' ta carry me ho-am."*

Again, they's a faint, distant light—blinkin' like a flashlight, now. Again, it seems to come from what I guess is the west. Yep, there it goes again. Maybe it's the Chawl-stin Lighthouse—but no, that be to the east, cross the harbor to Sullivan's Island. The only other lighthouse be the one to the southeast, on what's left of the sands of Morris Island, but that was abandoned years ago.

Still, wherever they's light a-shinin', they's sure to be people nearby, and so thinkin', I again set off for the distant, faint light. I trek and truck, trippin' twenty times before I finally arrive, all bung up, at a bungalow with only the two candlelit windows. The front door's wide open, throwin' out a luminescence that seems to draw me in.

I gingerly peek 'round the doorsill to see, sittin' against the wall along one length of the room, a row of black and white women all dressed in black and all sobbin' softly. 'Cross the room, along the length of the other wall, sits a row of somber men, also mixed, but all in black, emittin' a low harmonic hum in unison. This collective sound's the moanin' song I had heard and that directed me here.

At the far end of the room a young black girl sits on a bench, her back to the door. Before her they's a table, on which lays an oblong box. It's a coffin. They's havin' a wake in this house.

Before I can slip away, the young girl turns 'round, looks right at me.

"Why, Jim Aisle!" she hails me. "Come on in from the fog. It's all right."

What can I do? Where else can I go? All them people've seen me now. Well, maybe inside with the dead would be better, after all, than stayin' outside swallowed up by fog. I slowly walk up to the girl, sit down next to her. No one speaks; it's just the sobs and the baritone moans.

After what seems like hours, a big, robustious black man, with an abundant black beard coverin' he face, suddenly stands up to make an announcement.

"See here, we've had enough of the cryin', it's time for some flyin'. We need to fetch us a fiddle player to strike up a tune so's we can dance our brother home!"

"Oh, no," says the little girl sittin' aside me. "No need to do that. Why, this very night, we have in our company none other than the finest fiddler, not just in the Lowcountry, but in the whole of the two Carolinas! Here he is, Jim Aisle, hisself!"

My eyes go wide, my jaw drops, I try to swallow. "Me?" is all I can muster in reply.

"Oh, yes, you, Jim Aisle," says the little girl. "Now, don't make me out to be a liar before all these good people. Fetch you a fiddle, and let's have us a dance!"

Without a chance for another word, I get reeled 'round, and someone puts a fiddle and a bow in my hands. Then somehow, beyond my knowin', I strike up a lively tune that sets toes a-tappin' and hands a-clappin'. Everyone rises at once and begins a dance with a line-up that breaks up into pairs. The hoofers hike they heels waist-high as I fire up the fiddle, playin' on and on and on.

It's most likely these gymnastics will continue without a break, unless I can catch a break. Then a string breaks, soundin' like a sad cat, so I have to bring the music to an end. The women sit back down, and the men sit after. Then the big bearded fella stands up again.

"We need to send for the preacher-man and have a service here before day-clean. Y'know, they is a deadline." Everyone in the room nods in assent.

"No, wait," the little girl says. "No need to go get the good man out of his bed when we got us the finest lay preacher in the whole Holy City of Chawl-stin. Here he is, Brother Jim Aisle!"

"What?" I exclaim. "I can't run a service. I only visit church at Christmas and Easter. What do I know 'bout—"

To no avail, I can't avoid it, for somehow I have vestments put on me and a Bible placed in my hands. Two acolytes appear out of the crowd holdin' the burnin' candles from the windows. So, I solemnly conduct a memorial service for someone I don't even know, but the congregation congratulates me for the soothin' words with plenty of "Yes, yes!" and "Praise be!" blessin's.

Finally, everyone shouts a final "Amen!" and the air seems to settle. The sober acolytes take the Bible and vestments, lead me back to my seat, and replace the candles by the windows. An uncomfortable pause fills the room, and I wonder if now might be a good time to leave.

I start to get up, but the little girl pulls me back down. Instead, four other men stands up, walk over to the coffin and lift it up onto they shoulders. Now, three of the men be about average height, but the one fella be at least a head taller than the others. The coffin teeters between 'em at a cater-wonk angle, in danger of spillin' the cargo.

Now, I'm thinkin' what a shame it'd be if that poor stranger who we've just had such a fine service for and all, should wind up splayed out on the floor like some spastic tinker-toy statue. Of course, I can see this is a shared concern. The big bearded man calls out again.

"Awright, now, y'all. Is they a doctor in the house?"

Not a soul stirs in reply. Then everyone breaks out laughin'. The little girl waves 'em quiet.

"As a matter of fact," she explains, "right chere in this room we have a man of medicine with healin' abilities beyond the learnin' scope of modern science. Yes, and they ain't no other like him in the A-M-and-A."

All them mourners look at the little dark-haired girl like she's talkin' gibberish, or some dialect of it. She frowns. "Y'all know," she says, "the *All-knowin'* *Medicine* *Answermans.*"

The mourners sigh, nod they heads. "Oh yes, oh yes," some say.

I have a bad feelin' about this.

"And y'all know the good doctor, Jim Aisle!"

Every set of eyes in that long, gloomy room is a-starin' at me now.

"I don't know what to do," I protest, "or even where to begin doin' I don't know what!"

"You're too modest, you are, Jim Aisle," tsk-tsks the little girl. "Why, you're more successful than any of those doctors on TV."

All within the blink of an eye, I hold a very sharp scalpel in my latex-gloved hands. A pair of very long legs in dark pants are thrust before me. I point the blade, blink my eyes a few times, and cut about four inches off the shin bones.

Then with a *Pop! Pop!* the legs snap back into place, and the man springs up, no taller than the rest of the pallbearers. The four men take up the coffin again and head out the open door. The mourners all stand up, and pairin' off once more, they all follow in a long line. The little girl takes my arm and leads me.

She has to. I mean, if lost and in a fog was what I was before, I ain't even know then or now what track or trail I'm a-followin' in this funeral march through the marsh. They's twisty vines and gnarled oak tree roots all over the ground, yet we step right over 'em all. Only now, we's walkin' on pluff mud—*on* pluff mud—and that's just not possible. Pluff mud'll suck you down into the marsh up to your waist. The smell alone's enough to do ya in, if ya ain't from here. But they we be. And all the while, I'm evermore slappin' away wavin' fans of palmetto leaves. Finally, the line stops when we come to a wide tabby wall, about seven, eight feet high.

Maybe it surrounds a cemetery, but I guess they's no gate, 'cause the mourners starts a-climbin' over the wall, two by two. I'm all doubtful 'bout scalin' the wall; that tabby's made of crushed oyster shell, and I know I'm gonna scrape and cut my hands to pieces. Anyway, I follow the little girl, a-scramblin' up the wall and my hands don't the least bit get nicked. Now, I'm the last one on top of the wall. Just as I jump off, the wind cotch me like a pop fly, and whirls me and twirls me through the air. I gulp mouthfuls of cloud tryin' to shout, when I hit land suddenly, like the ground rush up to grab me.

I don't no more know where I be, what time it is, or nearly my own name. Yet, there I be—back at the cistern, with the lid still open. The full pail sits on the ground where I had placed it, with the water still shakin' and sloshin'.

"You got that wata?" yells the old duster woman from the doorstep of her hut of a house, not five steps away.

I just look at her with my mouth agape.

"Close that lid, if you're done," she commands.

I close my mouth and shut the cistern, pick up the pail, and follow her back inside. She takes the water from me, and goes to start a stew. The old man beckons me over to sit beside him again.

"Whatyasay?" he asks, hitchin' his suspenders over his shoulders. "Got you any more fish stories?"

"Hah!" I bark with a start.. "Funny you should say somethin' · like that. You won't believe what happened—" And I begin to sit down on the stool, but fall too far back, and never finish my sentence.

I awoke with my head and stomach feelin' like the twin weights of a dumbbell. Under my knees and my neck lay the two sacks of bundled, cut sweetgrass, and how *that* happened, I don't know. Sunshine washed my face. It was mornin', day-clean.

Slowly I stood up, achin' all over like I had been bronco-bustin' a nightmare. They was daylight aplenty, and I turned 'round and 'round lookin' for any evidence of the hut and the cistern, or the long wake-house, or the tabby graveyard wall, but they was nothin' there but me at Buzzard's Roost Point.

I grabbed the sacks filled with the severed sweetgrass, and they felt warm—too warm from just my body heat. The sacks seemed to radiate a heat from inside. I wasn't so sure I wanted the grass, now, after all.

"What the hey," I said to myself, decidin' to leave the sacks behind. I was too tired to mess with 'em anymore, and they'd be that much more I'd have to carry out. Besides, it's best to leave well enough alone. It was enough to have experienced whatever it was I had experienced, and survived to tell the tale.

Well-suh, tellin' the tale is what I've done ever since. Whether or not I am relatin' this biography or most any other story, folks tend to think that I have taken liberties with the verifiable. I cannot deny they confusion, but I cannot concur with they doubt. I was there, and saw and felt what I know. I revisit that trip every time I retell the story, and now, I've told it to you.

It may be that I was on a chosen path. It may be that I have been endowed with a special birthright. It may be that I am livin' a self-fulfillin' epithet.

Maybe it was the fried fish I ate.

"Maybe," I said to Jim. "Anyway, there sure is a lot to swallow with that story."

The Bad Business of Brave Bob

My fond friend Jim Aisle told a jump of a tale with this ghost story he said he raised from downtown Charleston.

They's a fella 'round chere we all know as "Brave Bob." That's 'cause he'd do most *anythin'* on a bet. Not that Bob was a gamblin' man, like in Las Vegas or out at the track, but the truth be told, he lived for the *dare*.

Brave Bob always landed on "cat's feet." Never a scratch did he suffer for all the somersault stunts and extreme endurance tests that other fool-hearted, faint-headed daredevils and ne'er-do-wells put him up to prove. Frenstance, they used to take Bob up I-26 to the exit at notorious Ashley Phosphate Road, referred to warmly by local motorists as "Ghastly Frustrate Road" for all the auto accidents along there.

Well-suh, they'd take a bandana, blindfold Bob, spin him 'round three times, shoot him across the interstate highway durin' rush-hour traffic. Now, I swear, as feet have inches, Brave Bob never ever got hit. No runs, hits, or errors.

Now they's a place, downtown Chawl-stin on Meetin' Street near Marion Square, a massive mansion where an elderly spinster lived alone. It's still there, a huge, handsome house for a little, little ol' lady to rattle 'round in and try to maintain. Must have been the overwork, constantly cleanin' the premises, that overtaxed her system, for the good lady passed away.

That left the house unoccupied. They was no one to leave the house to, no one to keep it up. Before long the paint would chip and peel here and there, a shutter or two would work loose and hang crooked, shingles would fall off the roof. It was prob'-ly punks who threw rocks through some of the windows. The whole place looked beat-up, and eat-up, and just plain sad.

Didn't take long for some scalawags to do the math, though. One, they's a deserted, dilapidated, and allegedly haunted house. Two, they's Brave Bob, who'll take on any dare. Three, why not add 'em together?

So a few of these late-night, low-rent rascals pooled a hundred dollars to bet Bob that he didn't have the sand to spend the night in that haunted house. Had to wait for the full moon, too, to insure that the spirits would be up and about. Bob said sure.

Now, this was in the middle of the summer, so Bob had to wait late for the sun to set before he could inaugurate the bet. He climbed in through one of the broken windows, to the back of the house. Inside, the furniture and effects were just as the old lady had left 'em, 'cept now everythin' wore a fine layer of dust or was otherwise cobwebbed-over.

It was good and dark in that lonely, maybe-haunted house, but Bob was brave, he wasn't concerned. He made hisself at home and relaxed, sittin' down on a divan to dine on his simple supper. After a while he yawned and stretched, then stepped upstairs to find a bed for the night.

In one room they was a four-poster, canopy rice bed that felt just right. Openin' onto the piazza—which is what we call a porch in Chawl-stin—was a pair of fancy French doors. They're real elegant 'cause they open down the middle, be half as wide as a regular door, and have lots of glass panes. Bob could easily see the full moon risin' in the clear night sky. He climbed into the bed, snuggled under the covers, and was soon sleepin' soundly.

Well-suh, it's the summertime down South, and in one of the most humid port cities on the coast. Sometimes, it's so steamy and uncomfortable that you can't sleep. It's as unbearable as insomnia, only it's in the air.

Brave Bob woke up in the middle of the night, all sweaty and suffocatin', so he threw off the covers. Only it was more like a snake sheddin' its skin. First unstickin' and peelin' off the sheets, then lettin' 'em slide to the floor.

That's when he saw it. Right there, at the foot of the bed. A pair of big white eyes starin' up at him out of the darkness. Bob didn't know what to think.

"Who is that?" he demanded to know. But no one answered. Nothin' stirred. Those white eyes stared at him, and Bob stared back.

"Who is that?" he demanded again, but nothin'. Just a pair of dead, white eyes, and a faint bumpy outline 'round 'em. Could be the head. Bob peered into the eerie dark.

Then he thought about it. It must be one of those ne'er-do-wells at the foot of the bed wearin' a Halloween monster mask of some kind. So, Bob reached under the pillow where he had planted his insurance policy for just such a situation. It was issued by the Smith & Wesson company and came in a .38 caliber.

Bob was whisperin' to hisself, "One more time I'll ask, and then, I can't be responsible for what follows." He looked down at those ghostly eyes and knobby head, and shouted, "Who is that?"

Still no one answered. No one jumped. Brave Bob pulled out that pistol, pulled back the hammer, pulled the trigger: *pow!*

"Yee-oww!" screamed Bob.

Well-suh, the way that silvery, full moonlight was a-shinin' across the piazza, through those French doors and into the bedroom, when Bob tore away the bed sheets he exposed his own feet, and darn, if he didn't shoot off his own big toe!

Bob musta thought his shiny moonlit toenails was the eyeballs of a boo-hag or some sucha thing. Ever after that, we always call him Hobblin' Bob. That's the truth. Some folks think that Hobblin' Bob is kin to Hoppin' John, but that there is a whole other story.

I said then to Jim, that he could serve up that heapin' helpin' for another time.

A Lowcountry Whale of a Tale

Jim Aisle told me a whale of a tale one afternoon as we walked the boards of the Folly Beach Pier, a fit setting for a fish tale.

Back before the comin' of the bo-it, that is, boat riders, that is, back before both the white folk and the black folk came to these pluff mud shores, when what are now the names of islands or ribbahs were the names of the peoples—Wando, Edisto, Wadmalaw, Kiawah—well-suh, these coastal settlements were sufferin' from a terrible drought. The crops were fewer, smaller, or failin' outright, and famine threatened. They was one particular boy named Ra-il (Get to the truth of the matter by spellin' it backwards!). He would always look out for his widowed grandmother, who kept her own home nearer the beach than the rest of the family and other villagers. She was always so jolly and fun to be with, it was magical, and Ra-il loved her for that. Now he worried about her survival.

So early one mornin' Ra-il skips breakfast, not that they's much to skip or break a fast with, and goes to his grandmother's house by the beach. She's inside her palmetto-thatched hut tendin' a cook fire, so he helps her place a pot of fresh water over the small flame.

"What will you cook, grandmother?"

"Whatever I have, as much as I need."

"I know, grandmother! I will go scout the rocks and dunes and scour the shore for you, and I will bring back a feast for a week!"

So down along the beach goes Ra-il with a fish net and a basket, but after a while he still hasn't seen so much as a seagull—and they're good scavengers. He's right discouraged and he thinks of quittin' but for his grandmother sittin' back home with only a pot of water over her cook fire. So he trudges on and on till he sees a shimmer-shine in a lagoon. There in the shallows is a school of silver mackerel. He thinks, enough for a meal easily, as his mouth waters. His hunger grows as he loosens the fish net. His belly begins barkin'. He throws the net and hauls in the catch.

Ra-il is so hungry he swallows the entire school of mackerel, whole; maybe that's where the expression, "Wholly Mackerel!" comes from. Anyway, it's so good, but he's still so hungry, and besides, he realizes he just ate his grandmother's breakfast. Then he spots shrimp scurryin' under the tiny waves, so he drops the net again and pulls in a catch of wrigglin' shrimp. Now y'all know it's a bona fide Lowcountry law that says you cannot ignore edible shrimp within arm's reach, so he lays down the law and lays into them shrimp. This is before cocktail sauce, too. His net is empty again, but his belly's full, for now.

Ra-il remembers his grandmother when over by the rocks juttin' out into the ocean he hears *Snap! Snap! Snap!* He scans the rocks and sees crabs, lots of crabs, snappin' they pincer claws, so he sneaks up and when the tide rolls in over 'em he casts the net. Again his cast is good and he hauls the captured crabs onto the sand, thinkin' 'bout crab salad and she-crab soup. He clips those crabs together by they pincers, opens his mouth wide, and swallows 'em: shells, feelers, claws, and all.

While Ra-il's midsection is expandin' progressively his grandmother-guilt gains weight on his shoulders, but he's still so very hungry and a little thirsty now, too, so he walks back to the water. Great googly-moogly! He sees all sorts of fish: cowfish, pigfish, sheepshead, bass, a whole set of drum, and he catches 'em each and every one and gobbles 'em down before you can say "starvin' grandma." Then he swims farther out to devour red snapper, bluefish, yellowfin tuna. He swallows swordfish and sail-fish, then a pod of porpoises, and finally a whole whale! He drinks down a boat-load of seawater, too.

Now Ra-il figures to go home to his grandmother, as big as he is and without a morsel for a meal. He's now bigger than any village it would take to raise him, so he'll never fit through the door of her hut, it's so small. She tells him in her jolly magical voice to climb in through the window, but that's smaller than the door, so she tells him to clamber up the roof and drop down the smoke hole, but that's smaller than the window. So she soothes his nerves and sort of sings to him to jump through the eye of a whale bone needle that she's holdin' up for him to see.

He laughs and takes a runnin' leap, the ground shakin' like an earthquake, but lo and behold, he sails through the eye of the needle and lands in the hot pot of water on the fire. They's a huge hissin' sound as steam envelops everythin', thunder roars overhead, the earth shakes one last time, and when the steam-fog lifts, they's no hut, no pot, no fire, no Ra-il, only his lonely grandmother. She comes to, lookin' all 'round her at nothin', then hears splashin' and runs to the shore.

In the shallows she sees mackerel, shrimp, and crabs. Splashin' through the breakers are cowfish, pigfish, sheepshead, bass, and drum. In smoother waves she sees red snapper, bluefish, yellowfin tuna, sailfish, and swordfish. Beyond 'em are the leapin', divin', dancin' dolphins, and at the horizon a whale spouts a salute, then dives down under. Ever after that the coastal folks, the Wando, Edisto, Wadmalaw, Kiawah, never feared Famine for they knew they could always fish a meal.

I couldn't hold it. I had to interrupt Jim and I blurted out, "Jim, that there's a whale of a tale!" He smiled, nodded, and said, "Yeah, that's a keeper. I guess that's the one that didn't get away!"

Lazy Lucky Lowcountry Jack

*Jim and I were lazing around one long afternoon, when he told me this
lovely fairy tale of labor.*

Luck has a way of followin' a person 'round, bidin' its time, till it
pounces upon some poor soul like stalked prey. Sometimes it
takes awhile to build up to that pounce, but when luck lands on
you, you'll know it. They was a hapless fella, nickname of Lazy
Jack, who once upon a postbellum time was livin' outside of
Chawl-stin in St. Andrews Parish—now West Ashley—with his
poor, widowed mama. They didn't have much, not after the
Federal tourist trade passed through Chawl-stin durin' this time
of so-called Reconstruction. Nonetheless, it was Jack's mama
who did all the worryin' as well as all the work, chore upon
chore, includin' the heavy liftin' and window-washin'. Lazy Jack
would spend most of his time inspectin' the insides of his eyelids
while sleep-testin' beds of all sorts: box-springs, hammocks,
haylofts, grassy hillsides. His was a demandin' occupation, full of
layoffs and dormant opportunities.

   While sittin' at Sunday supper, Jack's mama finally laid down
the law. She told him, "Jack, your luck has run out. Come the
mornin', I want you out of this house and employin' yo'self at

some honest satisfyin' trade. I can't have you layin' about, you lazy boy. I've toted the last load for you, Jack. You'll have to pay your own way if you're goin' to stay, that's all I'll say."

Well, on the one hand, Lazy Jack *couldn't* argue with his mama, and on the other hand he knew he *shouldn't* argue with his mama. So early Monday mornin', Jack set off towards Chawlstin to push his luck, find some honest work. He got hired as a day-laborer on a nearby government-confiscated plantation, helpin' to clear the fields for plantin'. It was hard, hot, long work, but at the end of the day, the foreman paid Jack a silver dollar coin with an eagle on either side. Jack took to pitchin' it up in the air . . . watchin' that coin a-glintin' in the sun . . . and catchin' it while he walked on home.

When he came to cross a creek, he traipsed across the boards placed there as a rude bridge, still a-pitchin' that silver piece in the air. Halfway across the creek, he missed his catch and the coin disappeared in the murky water. Just like that—*kerplunk!*—Jack lost his first honest day's wages.

"Jack! You lazy, careless boy!" Jack's mama said when he told her 'bout his day. "Tomorrow, if you get paid, put your pay in your pocket!"

"Tomorrow?" Jack said. "You mean I've got to go back to work again?"

"Yes, of course, son. Don't be silly," said Jack's mama. "One character flaw at a time, and you've been lazy long enough. Let's get you to workin' for a livin', first."

• • •

Bright and early Tuesday mornin' Jack once again set off from home to find work. Not wantin' to repeat his mistakes, he quickly passed by the newly cleared fields where he had toiled the day before and soon came to the pastures outlyin' Coburg Dairy. As luck would have it, Jack arrived as the cows were still standin' in they stalls, swollen and ready for milkin'. The dairyman was short some hands and he hired Jack on the spot.

All mornin' long Jack milked the cows of Coburg Dairy. He milked and he milked and he milked till they was no more milk to be milked that mornin'. Late in the afternoon he helped herd the cows in for they second daily milkin'. Jack milked and he milked and he milked some more till he hands were red and sore. The day's work done, Jack got paid not with coin, but with the frothy white "fruit" of his labor: a full canister of cool, fresh milk.

Now, Jack had to walk home as the sun met the dusk and he didn't care to measure the miles a carryin' his heavy liquid treasure. Then he recalled what his mama had said: "Put your pay in your pocket!" Bein' a good mama-lovin' son, Jack opened wide his pants pockets and poured out all the milk he'd been paid, first into one pocket and down his leg, and then into and down the other. He looked like he'd had an "accident," to put it politely. It was a lucky thing the light was fadin' or Jack would have been made a laughin'-stock by any eyewitness to his mess.

"Jack, you lazy, careless, foolish boy!" exclaimed his mama when he arrived home. "I see you followed my advice, but let me advise you now, that you are followin' too closely. Don't be so lazy, Jack, use your head. Use it for somethin' besides growin' hair on it, and carry your day's pay up on your noggin. Can you follow that, Jack?"

"Yes, mama, I can," Jack replied.

• • •

When Wednesday awoke Jack went back to the Coburg Dairy and was promoted—what luck!—to work in the creamery makin' butter and cheese. All mornin' long Jack separated the curds from the whey, and in the afternoon when his shift was done, he was paid with a fresh orange block of rich cheddar cheese. Followin' his mama's advice, Jack balanced the block on his head, and headed home.

The sun had not set yet, had hours to spare, as Jack walked home hot and sweaty. Or, at least at first Jack thought he was sweatin', but actually the block of cheddar cheese was a changin' from a solid to a liquid state and meltin' down his neck, under and over his shirt, and all down the rest of him. By the time he got home, Jack looked like human Velveeta.

"Jack! You lazy, careless, foolish, messy boy!" cried his mama. "How in the . . . what in the . . . oh, never mind, let's wash you off. And next time, son, just carry your pay in your own two hands. Grip it tight so you won't drop it, and hold it close to you."

"Yes, ma'am, I'll remember to do that," Jack assured her.

• • •

Jack decided that he'd had enough of dairy cows for now, so come Thursday mornin' he thought he would push his luck in the city of Chawl-stin. As he neared the Ashley Ribbah on the peninsular city's west side, he noticed several sailboats slidin' up and down the ribbah. A boat show was in town, anchored at the city marina, and sundry sailors were practicin' on the Ashley. The poor bridge man was havin' to open and close the drawbridge repeatedly for the water traffic. He needed help. It was just dumb luck that Jack showed up and offered to lend a hand. The bridge man was relieved and put Jack to work.

Throughout the day Jack watched the sailboats as he operated the mechanisms that drew the bridge. He daydreamed 'bout his own boat someday, a yacht perhaps, that he would use to cruise the coast. At the end of the day, for pay Jack chose one of the new kittens recently delivered by the bridge man's mama cat.

Jack firmly picked up the little furry kitty, clutched it to his chest, and set off for home. He tightly held the kitty and tried to stop its fidgetin', but it was fidgetin' from Jack's tight grip. Action, reaction. That kitty was all cat: out came the claws, and poor Jack was scratched, ripped, torn, bit, and hissed at till he threw out his arms lettin' go of the fiendish feline and yellin', "Scat!" The cat scat, but Jack's shirt was in shreds; his hands, arms, and face were scratched up and down and crossways.

"Oh, Jack! You lazy, careless, foolish, messy, torn-up boy!" his mama gasped. Jack explained, but she told him, "Jack, next time you get paid, here's what you do. Take a length of rope or strong string, tie it on, and pull it behind you. That way you won't get messed up, okay?"

"Okay, mama, I'll do just that," Jack affirmed.

• • •

Fresh again on Friday, Jack took off for town. He crossed the Ashley Ribbah Bridge when he came to it, tellin' the bridge man that he had to get downtown. Besides, Jack didn't want another cat. He made his way to the market and was able to hire on at Henry's Restaurant as a kitchen helper. All day long Jack was hoppin' like a frog on a skillet, from the mornin' preparations before openin', through the crush of the lunchtime mob, till after the dinner crowd had gone home. Before he left for home, the chef at Henry's gave Jack a whole ham for his day's pay. Jack had earned it, he told him with a wink. How lucky is that?

Of course, Jack dutifully remembered what his mama had told him to do, so he found a length of twine, tied it 'round the ham, then trailed it behind him through the streets of Chawl-stin and across the Ashley.

Every stray dog in the city followed Jack like he was some kind of savory Pied Piper. By the time he arrived home, they was no meat on the ham-bone. Even that wasn't worthy of the soup pot.

"Jack, you lazy, careless, foolish, messy, torn-up, bone-headed boy!" his mama yelled at him. "I don't know what I'm gonna do with you, son. You have a good heart, a strong arm, a broad back, but no sense a-tall! Tell you what, my lazy-headed Jack, next time carry your pay, whatever it is, up on your shoulders. At least it should all get home in one piece."

"Yes, mama, I will," Jack promised her.

Saturday Jack trekked back to the market. He had noticed the fine and fancy carriages that were rented out by liverymen from they stables near the Market, and he thought he might like to work with the horses and mules. After all, Jack had experience with livestock. He hired on for the day with Capall's Stables, a-leadin' the animals into they traces, cinchin' they straps, combin' they manes, feedin' 'em oats and carrots.

As Jack was unharnessin' a fussy mule, a sudden gust of wind caught the half-open stable door and slammed it shut with a tremendous *bang*! Several men threw theyselves to the ground thinkin' the War had restarted. That mule reared up, kicked out at Jack, and ran into the street, trailin' lines behind. People in the street ran up onto the sidewalks and people on the sidewalks ran into nearby stores as the frightened mule charged across the cobblestones.

Jack ran through the market vendors to head off the wayward mule. He leaped upon the mule's back and pulled it by the ears to stop before it careened into the graveyard at St.Philip's Church. Maybe Jack was blessed as well as lucky, but anyway, he saved the day.

For his pay—and to unburden hisself of a troublesome beast—Mr. Capall told Jack to keep the mule he saved. What a lucky break, now he could ride home. Only thing was, Jack's mama had given him explicit instructions on how to handle his wages, and he didn't want to disappoint his mama.

So, Jack got down under the belly of the beast, gathered its legs fore and aft, and lifted straight up. The poor mule found itself straddlin' Jack's shoulders as he went a-waverin', counter-balancin', and zigzaggin' down the street. Bystanders gave him a wide berth as he cut a haphazard path through the city.

Now, Lady Luck comes and goes like the tide, but sometimes she washes over a body near enough to drown him with good fortune. Jack was about to be in over his head, so to speak, mule and all.

At the corner of King and Queen Streets lived a one-time regional princess: a genteel Southern Belle named Gillian, the daughter of pedigree Chawls-tonians. Despite the death and destruction and destitute existence resultin' from 'the late unpleasantness,' her family's fortunes had not only kept afloat, but increased by benefit of blockade-runnin' brigantines. However, she stayed sad and forlorn, as lonely as she was lovely, because few beaus were available and she was untaken.

This sad-eyed Lady of the Lowcountry would sit daily on her piazza, watchin' the traffic at the royal corners of her relative realm. It had been seven sad years without a single smile from her, let alone a loud, lusty laugh. Her mama worried over her, as any mama would; but her daddy was a gamblin' man who put up stakes worth a fifth of his fortune, includin' the pick of any of his fleet of ships. The favorable prospect of matrimony to his daughter naturally followed.

All that any worthy man who applied hisself had to do was to make daddy's li'l princess laugh. He would have to make her laugh and laugh and laugh—make her merry and break her blues. Then, with any luck, hopefully he'd have a Happily Ever After.

• • •

While Gillian glumly sat on her piazza, Jack meandered down Meetin' Street, lurchin' lazily, then swung quickly down Queen Street. At first Gillian didn't believe what she thought she saw: a man and a mule comin' down the street, but somehow upside down? As she stared she recognized that indeed a man and a mule were approachin', and yes, they were mixed up, and oh, it looked silly. She smiled slightly, softly, and slowly shook her head as Jack danced like a drunken sailor, a-totin' livestock.

Gillian began a-titterin' and a-snickerin', a-teeheein' and a-gigglin', till finally a full-fledged guffaw of ha-ha-ha-ha exploded from her throat. Her mama and daddy heard her gleeful cries and ran to her in both joy and trepidation. Then they saw Jack.

As native Chawls-tonians, they enjoyed a good story, and surely, the sight of man and mule—in that order—a-strugglin' down the street provided fodder for they daughter to return to 'em like a happy endin'. Naturally, as luck would have it, Jack was welcomed into the home and hearts of Gillian's family. Before long, they courtship well-affirmed, they wed, and were set up handsomely with both dowry and Jack's winnin's from the wooin'. What a lucky guy!

Most rewardin' of all: Jack never had to work another day in his life!

• • •

Well, Jack was able to provide for his poor mama all the rest of her days. From the fine fleet of his father-in-law, Jack picked out a fit ship for his own, learned to sail it well. Then Jack and Gillian cruised the coast, enjoyin' the style of the sea-farin' life. They finally settled down, though, in northern Florida, by the St. Johns Ribbah.

There, Jack and Gillian spread they wealth 'round, bein' generous and all, settin' up hospitals, libraries, art galleries, museums, schools, parks, highways. The people there in north Florida thought so highly of Jack—'specially whenever he told the story of how he and Gillian met—that they decided to honor him, and they own associated good luck, by namin' they hometown, now a city, after him.

Surely you've heard of Jack's-own-ville, Florida?

I told Jim that I have heard of a lot of things in my time, some true, some not, and this is certainly one of them.

Cold as the Grave

Jim told me about the strange death of one Billy Porcher, but not for any particular reason but that Jim is always conversing on points of interest. This time he was pointing at Lowcountry ghost legends.

It was back in the time of our forefathers—that is, the four fathers of South Carolina, y'know, Sumter, Marion, Pickens, and Rutledge—and they was a Mr. Samuel Ravenel, who had a rice plantation up the Ashley Ribbah. He also had a beautiful, robust, but pertinacious young daughter, Sally. She was of an age to marry a peer, another of the planter class, as her father earnestly believed things ought to be. But Sally had her eyes already starcrossed and set on Billy Porcher, the chisel-chinned, broadshouldered, God-fearin' son of a yeoman farmer, and hisself employed as one of Mr. Ravenel's stable hands.

But Mr. Ravenel wouldn't have that. He wouldn't let his daughter marry beneath her station. He was just lookin' out for his daughter, as any daddy would. It was a ticklish situation, but Mr. Ravenel was gonna take a stand, based on his beliefs and what he thought he knew. He was declarin' war on true love. Now, they's been a lot of talk lately in the news about what they call WMD, the Weapons of Mass Destruction. Well, Mr. Ravenel was fearful for Sally's future, so this was a case of NWMD, or Not With My Daughter! And you'd better believe it. Nevertheless, Sally herself was resolute, and folks could tell how Sally and Billy were fated.

Finally, Mr. Ravenel marooned Sally with some of his kin out to John Island, but he whisked her away so sudden that Billy didn't know where she went and could only think she'd abandoned him. After that, Billy moped and moaned, threw off all work, and within two weeks had taken to sick bed and died.

Mr. Ravenel soon heard folks speculate how Billy had died of a true-love's broken heart over missin' Sally, and he felt somewhat responsible, if it was true. Still, Sally didn't know 'bout any of this. Till one evenin', the day after Billy's funeral, she was pensively gazin' out from the piazza of her kinfolk's big house when she spotted a lone rider comin' down the lane. It was Billy, no mistake. He was astride one of her daddy's prize mares.

"Sally, I've come to see you, to be with you one last time."

"I'm so glad you've come, Billy, but what do you mean by one last time?"

"Come, ride with me now."

"Ride? Where to?"

"Ride on home, Sally, with me now."

"Why? Is everythin' all right? How's daddy?"

"He wants me to fetch you home, m'love."

"Well . . . wait. I'll collect a bag—"

So the stable groom and his would-be bride rode homeward under moon glow. Sally held on tightly to her beloved Billy, and ran her fingers through his hair. She brushed 'em across his forehead and felt a coldness, a dampness, an ailment.

"Why, Billy, are you well? You might be chilled. You feel as cold as the grave."

But he said nothin', so she pulled out from her bag a bandana of indigo blue and patterned with crescent moons. She fashioned it into headwear and wrapped it over Billy's crown while they rode on and on into the night.

Two hours before cock's crow, they arrived at the Ravenel

plantation. Sally alit and ran into the house callin' for her father. He awoke and asked her why had she come home, and at this hour? She mentioned Billy, but Mr. Ravenel objected, said that was impossible, so she led him to the front yard. Billy wasn't there. Nor was the horse, but they found it in the stable, still saddled and sweatin' hard. But Billy wasn't there, either. Then Mr. Ravenel told Sally what he knew of Billy's demise. She disbelieved him.

"Oh, Daddy, that's just some Halloween prank y'all dreamt up. I won't believe Billy's dead lest I see his body in a box pulled out of the ground!"

Well, like they say, she wouldn't crawfish from it, her mind was set. Her daddy knew how obstinate she could be; she'd never falter in assertin' herself. They was nothin' for it but to go wake up Billy's folks and run through the whole argument anew, till his ma and pa could only gape in a state of predawn sleep and awe at the strong-willed love Sally held in her heart for Billy.

They gathered some shovels and a lantern and carried over to the Porcher family graveyard, enclosed by a picket fence and sparrowgrass. At a fresh plot they dug and dug till they hit wood, cleared out the coffin, pulled it out of the ground, and lifted off the lid. There in the coffin lay Billy dead, as cold as clay. 'Round his head was that crescent-patterned indigo blue bandana that Sally had put there that very night.

When I caught my breath, I questioned Jim about the veracity of his account. He replied, "I don't lie, you just have to wait for the right combination of facts." I couldn't argue with that.

Mr. and Mrs. Vinaigrette

My friend the storyteller, Jim Aisle, who is said to be the Lowcountry Liar, told me this sweet and sour tale of two sillies.

Mr. and Mrs. Vinaigrette lived in a cruet bottle. It had a fine swan neck, and was made of thin green glass. That might seem like an impossibility, but when two people are so compatible and content, so comfortably confident in theyselves as Mr. and Mrs. Vinaigrette, then nothin' is impossible. Besides, nobody else was willin' to live in a cruet bottle.

As a complementary couple, Herb and Olive Vinaigrette divided they time together. He liked to work out in the garden, tendin' to the weeds, and encouragin' the greens. She liked to work indoors, and was forever fastidiously cleanin' and straightenin' to make a pleasant home under the glass. They would wave to each other often durin' the day while they worked.

One fateful afternoon, Herb is wavin' to Olive, then he doffs his cap and bows. In turn, she stops sweepin' and curtsies by fannin' her skirt and dippin' quickly. When she does, she also drops the broom, the handle strikes the glass with a hard knock, and cracks are sent racin' across the cruet. Then the thin glass shatters and falls to pieces 'round her.

"Great googly-moogly!" cries Mr. Vinaigrette. "Are you all right, Olive, honey?"

"Yes, I am, Herb, dear," she replies. "But the house is an absolute wreck. I'll never be able to tidy up."

"They's only the door to guard, anymore," he comments. "It's the only thing left standin'."

"Well, it will be dark soon, too, my sweet," she says, "and we can't stay here for the night."

"No, darlin'," he agrees, "we can't now."

Despite the sudden sad loss of they fragile home, Herb and Olive surmise that it'd be senseless to shed tears over such a sour situation. It be just another vintage case of the same ol', same ol', so why worry whinin' 'bout it? Instead, the seasoned Vinaigrettes would find a brand new bottle together.

They share a sigh, then shoulder they loads. Mr. Vinaigrette grabs the door, and balancin' it upon he back, steps off down the road to find a new home. Mrs. Vinaigrette collects a few odds and ends, and gathers some of the ripe produce from the garden for the trek.

By sundown, they are still on the road—down by Savage Road, in fact—not yet to a secure shelter, but too far gone to turn back. Before much longer they truly will be in the dark, and likely to get good and lost till who knows when they might be found. So they decide to spend the night in a nearby magnolia tree.

They haul up the door and brace it between branches to serve as a bed. Up there in the air should keep 'em safe from wild beasts and wilder boogymen. By dusk they are settled down up above and as snug as they can be in a tree.

Before long, they hear voices, and all of a sudden, they's a gang of raucous robbers gathered 'round the magnolia tree. The tree be a rendezvous point where local thieves regularly split up the spoils of ill-gotten goods. Mr. and Mrs. Vinaigrette huddle together tremblin' in fear. What if they are discovered? What would these nasty thieves do?

The Vinaigrettes shake and shiver so much, the door works loose and comes crashin' down on the den of thieves. The robbers all run off screamin' into the darkness, and not a one of 'em returns that night. The Vinaigrettes are so mixed up, they don't stir till mornin'.

That's when they find the loot left behind by the scared-off robbers. They's a worn brown leather bag with a broken brass clasp—not that it could close anyway, for all the dollar bills stuffed into and spillin' out of the bag. It be a satchel of paper money.

"Great googly-moogly!" the Vinaigrettes cry together.

"We're rich," says Olive.

"It's a mighty fine find," says Herb.

"We can buy any kind of bottle we like now. How 'bout considerin' one of those big office water coolers?"

"Maybe so, but I'd probably have to buy it in downtown Chawl-stin, darlin'. That could take all day to get there, get it, and get back here."

"Well, why don't you go get us a bottle, and I'll guard the door. All right, sweetie?"

So Mr. Vinaigrette picks up the satchel of paper money and heads off down the road to Chawl-stin. Near the pastures of Coburg Dairy Mr. Vinaigrette meets a dairy farmer with the name "Dale" stitched onto his ball cap, who is out standin' in his field with several milk cows. Dale eagerly sells a big brown bossy milk cow in a sweet deal to Mr. Vinaigrette. It's an even swap for the whole satchel, and Mr. Vinaigrette is sold solid on Dale's deal.

"Great googly-moogly! Think of all the milk we'll have! Regular, two percent, skim, butter. And cheeses. And ice cream. Oh, how sweet for sweet Olive!"

On the way back, Mr. Vinaigrette meets a young boy pullin' three little squealin' piglets along a length of rope. The more they pull, the more they squeal and the redder they get, in shades from pink to magenta. They almost entangle the cow, who moos.

"Great googly-moogly!" cries Mr. Vinaigrette. "What kind of swine—"

"You can have 'em, anytime," says the young boy. "If you'd part with that cow, now, I could swap you. I'm takin' these three down to the Chawl-stin Market, but you could save me the trip. What do you say?"

"I'd say first what's your name, son, and where you from?"

"My name is Jack, sir. I work on a pig farm near Bacon's Bridge Road, and I've been sellin' pigs all the way to Chawl-stin today. This is my last set of piglets. They's great little squealers, but after they been properly fattened up and grown up, they'll make prime wholesome hogs."

"Prime swine? Mine? Great googly-moogly!"

"Yessuh, and besides, that's three times as much pig as you have of cow, now."

"That's a fact," nods Mr. Vinaigrette. "Okay, I'll swap."

"What a sweet deal," Jack says, and thinks to hisself how his mama didn't think he knew beans 'bout business transactions.

Just like that, Mr. Vinaigrette doubles his square footage, even though somehow the math doesn't seem to add up. So, stuck with the three squealers, he sets off down the road again. He has his mind on bacon and blue ribbons.

After an hour of followin' the wigglin' piglets, Mr. Vinaigrette hears music up 'round the bend. Sittin' comfortably in the shade of a dogwood tree, a bearded man is playin' a guitar. The piglets settle down, and after a moment they are sound asleep.

"Great googly-moogly," whispers Mr. Vinaigrette. "How did you do that?"

"Well, partly it's the instrument, and it's partly what you play. Do you play, Mr.—?"

"Vinaigrette. Uh, no, I don't play, but I sure would like to learn. My wife would be so pleased to hear such sweet music."

"Oh, yeah? By the way, my name is Fox, Frank Fox. I'll tell you plain, Mr. Vinaigrette, not only do I play guitar, but I can eat, too, and I am hungry. I could maybe part with this guitar if you'd be willin' to trade your piglets? How 'bout it?"

"I don't know. I had the one cow, and now I have the three pigs—"

"Well, this here is a six-string guitar."

"Why, that's twice as good, and even better!"

"I'll say."

"Sweet honey of the Rock, I'll do it. Mr. Fox, I'll trade you these three little piglets for your magical six-string guitar. Here and now, I say, take it or leave it."

"Say no more. Let's shake on it. I'll even throw in an extra C chord for free."

"I can't say no to that!" exclaims Mr. Vinaigrette, and seals the deal.

So now with the six-string slung over his shoulder, tryin' to serenade the scenery as he hikes along the highway, Mr. Vinaigrette only blisters his fingers while the midday sun over-head blisters everythin' else. After an hour of too much sweat for the toil, Mr. Vinaigrette gives up his dream of a duet with his wife, as *Olive and Herb*. This guitar work is too complicated to play; it has six strings and he has only the four fingers, although he feels like he's all thumbs. After all, it's too hot to walk, so for a little rest he finds some shade under a large oak tree at a cross-roads.

Shortly thereafter, along comes a slim black youth wearin' a brimless golf cap, totin' a big black bumbershoot, and whistlin'. He hails Mr. Vinaigrette, who motions him over to sit a minute in the shade, and maybe trade. That umbrella looks temptin'.

Turns out, the fella's name is Robert Johnson. He's on his way to work another day as a caddy, but he prefers music to golf, even though he doesn't yet play any instrument. Mr. Vinaigrette becomes inspired, and right there at that crossroads under the heat and glare of the midday sun, he trades to a young Robert Johnson his very first guitar for an old, used umbrella.

After that, with the umbrella open, makin' mobile shade for hisself, Mr. Vinaigrette happily travels along the trail on his way back home. Happy he is till he realizes that the various and sundry birds roostin' here and there on branches overhead along the trail seem to have a collectively accurate, if not uncanny, knack for hittin' a movin' target below. *Bombs away!* Soon bird poop covers the bumbershoot.

So Mr. Vinaigrette tries to shake off the slop by repeatedly closin' and openin' the umbrella. They's a sharp snap and it inverts to a cone. Tryin' to push-pull the mechanism on the spine, then proppin' it against the fork of a tree and pressin' steadily, Mr. Vinaigrette finally forces the umbrella back through, breakin' three of the struts, bendin' the spine, and tearin' the cloth in two places. It is a prize to behold.

So what does he have to show Olive for his busy day of business? He started with a satchel of paper money, bought a big brown bossy Coburg Dairy milk cow, traded her for three little wiggly piglets, swapped 'em for a fine finger-stretchin' six-string guitar, and gave that away for a perfectly utilitarian umbrella. Yet, for all these mercantile maneuvers, Mr. Vinaigrette now holds only a half-inverted, half-reverted, spine-bent, cloth-rent, bird-poop-bespackled, used-to-be umbrella.

He arrives back to the clearin' by the big magnolia tree, and Olive is still guardin' the door. She's overjoyed to see him, and her joy turns to mirth as he tells her of his travails that day. Together they share a hard laugh between they soft hearts.

It must not have been too long after this that I last saw Mr. and Mrs. Vinaigrette. They been walkin' along the side of the road, still totin' the door—guardin' it for dear life—and headed up Highway 61 to Summerville, or somewhere else in Dorchester County. The last I heard of 'em was clear up in the hills of east Tennessee. For all I know, that's where they went, if not stayed. Who knows, maybe they changed they name and settled down happily ever after in a Mason jar.

I told Jim that the story of the Vinaigrettes has a sweet ending for folks in such a pickle.

The Wreck-Construction of the Ashley Ribbah Bridge

As a historian, my wayfaring friend Jim Aisle never lets the facts get in the way of a good story like this one, which he says has spanned the ages.

Well-suh, tomorrow is the annual Cuppah Ribbah Bridge Run. Y'all ready, set to go? It'll be good, healthy fun, but it'll be hard work, too. Y'know, they's a few reasons why the Cuppah Ribbah Bridge, the ol' Grace Memorial, of all the bridges spannin' Chawl-stin, is the one used for this high falutin' foot race.

The official distance of the race is ten kilometers, and the bridge itself takes up a coupla those klicks, as they call 'em. Either way, it's a full English mile. Add to that the rollercoaster rise and dip of the bridge road itself, all suspended in a high arc to allow ships to pass beneath, till you run down the long incline into Chawl-stin, through the heart of downtown, and end the race at Ansonborough Field. After you've made it there, you can re-view the Cuppah Ribbah Bridge itself, and compare your individual accomplishment with other runners. It's a challengin' course, but it's a friendly competition, and really, you're measurin' yourself.

They's another reason, rarely mentioned, why the bridge run is held over the Cuppah Ribbah. That's because of the buried rumor, based on fact, about the barely known story concernin' the reconstruction of the old, original Ashley Ribbah Bridge. It's said the very devil was in the work.

It was about a fortnight after Appomattox, in April of eighteen and sixty-five. The Yankees already had invaded the peninsula city in February—a year to the day since the Southern submarine, the CSS *Hunley*, sank the USS *Housatonic*. It was a devil of a time, too, durin' which the Yankees yanked out all the stops by bombardin' the city of Chawl-stin. They gave a whole new look to the Holy City with its many churches; now it looked more like the hole-y city.

Anyway, as of February the Confederates had fled to the west, across the Ashley Ribbah, and had wrecked the bridge there at both banks to make it impassable. Add to that damage the subtraction of one of the four towers at the bridge-draws that had been shot away by Yankee shellin'. Now in April, with the war officially over, there still stood an unconnected causeway, a very unattractive drawbridge.

Now, no one could cross the Ashley Ribbah without a bo-it. No one could use a bo-it without gettin' shot at or arrested by the soldiers. That's how things stood.

Notwithstandin' the four years of wearin', tearin' war that had passed over the bridge, the civilian townsfolk were determined to rebuild it theyselves. They did not want that authority under army control, so a secret meetin' was set where a discussion was held over the fate of the span. They was a large crowd of concerned citizens drawn from all over Chawl-stin—a mix of ex-slaves and bluebloods mostly, but few able-bodied yeomen artisans fully fledged to build a bridge. Those qualified had fled or were dead.

Except for Pluff Mud Pete. He was a typically hospitable Southerner, a denizen of the Lowcountry environment, a Chawl-stin character of immutable integrity—but he smelled bad. Pluff Mud Pete had attained his moniker from the telltale aroma of his person, a redolent essence reminiscent of the salt marshes surroundin' the city.

On the other hand, Pete was such a handyman, a true Jack-of-all-trades, who could make or reshape 'most anythin', who was as much an artist as artisan, who always had a nice smile and a kind word for everyone he met, or would give you the shirt off his back, and never complained. Despite his overwhelmin' presence as the salt-marsh-of-the-earth, he was an admired, if not overly cherished, member of the community. He, too, had been through Hell and high water durin' the war, but he, too, had survived and had helped others prevail. Now he, too, faced this new crisis that arose before Chawl-stin.

At the meetin', several people stood up to opine, some at the same time, but eventually everyone was heard. They was pro and con from here to yon, with some valid, some vainglorious, solutions. When all the speakers had a say, without any decisions made, the crowd cleared a space to let Pete speak.

"Go ahead, Pete, tell us what you think!"

"Your word's good enough for us, Pete!"

Pete rubbed his stubbly chin, scannin' the crowd. These folks were angry and anguished, fueled by frustration, and Pete was not sure that he could fix that. He only knew what he could do.

"Let's take a good look at the bridge in the mornin'," he said. "Give it a first-rate inspection, see what's what. We can't fix nothin' in the dark. For now, y'all go home and rest. Get a good night's sleep. We'll meet at the bridge come day-clean."

That was the only thing that everyone could agree to do. The meetin' broke up. Everyone went home.

• • •

Next mornin' after curfew, a coupla few dozen Chawls-tonians showed up where the old Ferry Road stopped abruptly at the blasted-out bank of the Ashley Ribbah. The bridge, or what was left of it, was in sad, sorry shape. No one could reach the island safely where the drawbridge itself stood, nor was they much point in raisin' the draws anyway, since the channel was so choked with debris no deep draft craft could pass upstream.

Despite the dangerous debris, and without regard to the restrictions emplaced by the army authorities, they be Pluff Mud Pete hisself, ever more a-rowin' his own johnbo-it from midstream. He slipped up onto the shore, secured the line, and scrambled up to meet the gathered crowd.

"It's gonna need some work," he told 'em. "Long, difficult, heavy-liftin' work. I'm a stone mason, among other things, as y'all know, but they's more work here than I could manage in a lifetime."

The townsfolk were dismayed. Some had prayed over the repair of the bridge, and those who had not yet come to that point now began to think of addin' they voices to the plea. A few fell to they knees. Uncertainty was astir in the minds of the citizens. Doom was afoot in the hopeless hearts of some.

Just then, a tall gentleman called out from the back of the crowd, and began to make his way to the bank. This fine gentleman was hisself a sight to behold. He was tall and straight as a church steeple. His clothin', brocaded here, satin there, designated him as a person of importance, wealth, and power, yet he walked with a telltale limp.

For support, he leaned on an elegant ebony cane with a gold knob handle. The cane was flawless and shiny—a black stick bright as a mirror. As the gentleman moved, the cane caught the sun but a split second to shine a blindin' bolt of light into the eyes of bystanders. The townsfolk could barely blink in the brilliance.

"Ladies and Gentleman, good citizens of Chawl-stin!" he announced, ingratiatin' the congregation with his pronunciation. "May I, perhaps, be of assistance here?"

Folks was skeptical. This fella was a stranger, not a native, no one knew him. Durin' times of such duress who knows what kind of strange bird might fly in? This strange stranger had all about him the smell and smugness of a contemptuous, scalawag carpetbagger.

"I am not from here, I am a travelin' businessman," he began, "although I have visited your fair city before. I noticed the mournful condition of your one and only bridge, here. Alas, the Ashley River Bridge. . . . ahh, yes, war *is* Hell, if I do say so myself. You can quote me. I'm sure you good people will agree with me, that this is a most *uncivil* war. Aah, look at the state of this dis-union. Look at the condition of your bridge! I dare say, I do believe I can take you out of this dire plight."

Everyone perked up they ears and gave the well-dressed, well-spoken stranger they undivided attention. No one spoke but him. Pete arched his brows and stroked his chin, a-listenin'.

"I have a wide and varied background," continued the stranger, "and I am a fully qualified professional in everythin' that I do. I waste nothin'. My work is guaranteed, one thousand per-cent!"

"Can you really fix the bridge?" asked someone.

"How long will it take?" asked someone else.

"What other work have you done?" asked Pete, pointedly.

The stranger said, "Well, now, I don't wish to brag—"

"It ain't braggin' if you really done it," said Pete.

"All right then. I'll tell you a little about my past projects. I think you will all be suitably impressed. Then, I believe, we can get down to business."

The stranger twirled his cane, shootin' bright light off the sun. He took a breath and raised hisself up a head taller. He smiled a wide smile while scannin' the crowd.

"I have been in the enterprise of gainful employment for quite some time," he said, and tapped his cane. "I have employed many others before now, and have gained from the enterprise. For instance, there is the London Bridge."

"Didn't they rebuild it some time back?" asked a citizen.

"Yes, some thirty-odd years ago," answered the stranger. "They also tore down the old stone bridge. Truly, I did not have anythin' to do with it fallin' down."

"Sounds like a nursery rhyme to me," muttered Pete.

"All right then," snapped the stranger, a little bit stung. "Uh, I mean, pardon me, I can understand your skepticism, but I have verifiable credentials. I have been at this work for quite some time. I, heh, honestly don't know when I signed my first contract, but one of my earliest construction jobs was the Great Wall of China."

"You did repair work on the Great Wall of China?" asked another citizen.

"No, I helped persuade the Emperor that he needed a long, strong wall built across the country that would stop invaders and protect the people. Just like now, it was a necessity. Y'know, keep the bad out, keep the good in."

"You can keep the good out, the bad in, too, with a wall," commented Pete. "That's no guarantee."

"Uh, well, yes, perhaps," said the stranger, a little flustered. "I convinced the Chinese Emperor nonetheless, and the Wall still stands. Good or bad, in or out, you are each free to choose how you look at it, and what you make of it."

"Speakin' of freedom," replied Pete, "how 'bout that bridge up there in Concord, y'know, ninety years ago? You have anythin' to do with that?"

"Oh, no, no, no," the stranger chuckled. "That Shot Heard 'Round the World was purely Divine Providence at work. Although, I did first arrive here later on to ride through the South with my protégé, Colonel Tarleton."

"You mean Bloody Ban?" cried an old man.

"You say, Tarleton's Quarter?" cried another.

"Which was no quarter at all?" asked the stranger in answer. His smile grew wider. "Yes, and yes. We never did catch your Swamp Fox, though I tried—"

"Like the Devil?" asked Pete.

"Ha ha, yes, you certainly can say that!" the stranger exclaimed. "As a matter of fact, until just this mornin' when my mount was confiscated by the martial authorities, I had been ridin' alongside General Sherman himself!"

They was stone silence. No one moved. They barely breathed.

"Now, about your bridge," the stranger began again. "I will have it repaired for you, for a relative fee, naturally."

At that the crowd began to smile, chuckle, laugh. No one had enough, if any, real money. Family jewelry or heirloom silver was about all anyone in Chawl-stin had to barter with, and the last person they wished to engage in business was anyone allied to the Yankee occupation. The Devil hisself wasn't even on that despicable list.

"Of course, that don't mean you'll just take cash," observed Pete.

"Of course not," replied the stranger. "Naturally, I deal in all manner of commerce, and there is a slidin' scale to value. My payment is simple; it only requires a single installment. I merely request the mortal soul of the first person to cross the bridge. Isn't that a fair exchange?"

Again, they was a stony silence. No one cared to be the first to cross, and therefore, become the last for any kind of salvation. Yet everyone in Chawl-stin had come to that bridge, and now had to cross it. One way or another.

"All right, then, Ol' Scratch," Pete addressed the stranger. "Just how long will it take you to repair the bridge?"

"Would twenty-four hours be too soon?" the Devil teased, tapping his cane in the dust.

"Twenty-four hours?" said several citizens.

"It will take just one day, then the Piper gets paid," sang the Devil.

What to do? On the one hand, the townsfolk had to rebuild the bridge, and quickly, if only to maintain a presence, a community, in spite of—and to spite—an encroachin' army. On the other hand, nobody knew who amongst 'em was willin' to sacrifice his or her only soul to the Devil, forever, albeit to the everlastin' benefit of others, even strangers.

"Folks!" volunteered Pete. "Seems to me we're stuck between the wreck of our stone bridge and the hard fact of choosin' the fool to cross first. Don't nobody need to step forward."

"But what can we do, Pete?"

"After all, he's the Devil!"

"That's a fact, a verifiable fact," consented Pete. "Howsomever, if we all go ahead and let the Devil hisself here repair the bridge, don't y'all know that our otherwise occupyin' federal friends are sure to notice such a feat, and come a-runnin'? There and fore, I propose, whereas our innate Southern hospitality mandates that we should let bygones be bygones, then by all means we should all accede to the Union, and allow the Yankees to have the honor of bein' the first to, ah, cross over. Whatch y'all think?"

Without hesitation the crowd of Chawls-tonians cheered a chorus of approvals. The Devil nodded his head vigorously, and leanin' on his cane, tapped the toe of his boot on the ground like a he-goat bouncin' his back hoof before a head-buttin' charge. Pete touched his thumb to his nose, and pursed his lips, then said, "Well, Mr. uh, say, Ol' Scratch, just what should we call you?"

"Ha, why not for this occasion, call me Mr. Spann. Ha-ha-ha-ha-ha!"

"That'll do," agreed Pete. "So now, Mr. Spann, you say we can all leave right now with the peace of mind that you will fulfill a contract to reconstruct this here bridge by this time tomorrow, and at which time, you will collect the mortal soul of the first person to cross said bridge. That 'bout right?"

"In a nutshell. There is only the small, but formal matter of a signed contract between the principal parties. That would be myself, and you, perhaps, sir, as a local, vocal representative. Are you game, sir?" Mr. Spann airily raised his nose a snoot higher.

Pluff Mud Pete was made of sterner stuff, and certainly would not be outdone, even by the Devil incarnate. However, Pete was never gonna endorse a soul-bindin', blood-signin' contract, not for anyone's sake. He realized how relieved his neighbors would be if only he made the deal with the Devil, so he came to a compromise.

"On one condition," Pete said. "No blood-lettin'. I'll make my mark, but I'll only make my mark in pluff mud! You cotton to that, Mr. Spann?"

"I believe that will do. Anyway, it will at least set a precedent in any court in the country, I'm sure. Heh heh heh. By the way, what exactly is this pluff mud that you mentioned?"

Smilin' an apple-cheeked grin, Pete made his way down the bank to scoop up a handful of the goop. It was but a small sample of Lowcountry soul in the soupy soil. He came back to slap the glop into Mr. Spann's open hands. Spann inspected the taupe-colored, quicksand-thick pluff mud. He deeply inhaled its odor—its unbelievably rich stench of sea salt, swamp, and sun-baked shore—and gagged.

Regainin' his composure, Mr. Spann spat out, "Man, oh, man, does that ever clear the sinuses! All right, then, we shall sign, in this!"

With that, he snapped his fingers and his wrist—*poof!*—to produce a gold-seal-embossed printed document, full of upper-case Whereases and Therefores. He plopped the pluff mud onto the bottom of the document, then he and Pete placed they left thumbs on the muck to make they marks and seal the deal. Mr. Spann's spot sizzled, and a wisp of gray smoke arose from it. Pete winked.

"Now y'all know to stay away from here, 'specially from black-dark to day-clean!" proclaimed Pete. "We'll let the Dev— I mean, Mr. Spann, here, do his work. Tonight, he'll be plenty busy, so y'all can rest real easy. Sleep is at a premium these days."

That was a tantalizin' offer few folks could refuse. The crowd broke up, its individuals goin' about they own daily business, puttin' the business of the bridge behind 'em. Pete tipped his hat at Mr. Spann, climbed down to his johnbo-it, and slipped upstream with the tide. Mr. Spann rolled up the document, put it snugly in a coat pocket, and disappeared with another snap of his fingers.

• • •

That night, sometime between sleepin' and wakin', the Devil as Mr. Spann did his work over the troubled waters of the Ashley

Ribbah. Come mornin', after the cock's crow and curfew, the crowd came again, with many more curious Chawls-tonians to bear witness. None were disappointed.

Lo and behold! They was an intact, in place, fully functional drawbridge a-spannin' the Ashley Ribbah. It looked sturdier than the former structure, and fairly gleamed in the sunshine. Everyone was amazed and proud. They began to compliment theyselves on the cleverness of they collective decision, and to boast about beatin' the Yankees. Now, sure, let the Yankees come!

Just then, a voice was heard callin' from across the ribbah on the far bank. It was Pluff Mud Pete. He was wavin' and callin' out to the townsfolk on the town-side bank. Nobody spotted his bo-it, but somehow, he was already on the other side, and sure-ly, he did not already walk across the bridge!

Mr. Spann was suddenly among the onlookers, towerin' above 'em but unheeded, as everyone was strainin' to hear what-ever Pete was shoutin' about from the other shore. Step by cane step, Mr. Spann approached the foot of the bridge and inched his way to the edge. His hearin' was keen, his eyesight sharp; what he could not hear, he would read from afar.

"Sinkhole!" Pete shouted. "They's a sinkhole over here!"

"STINK BOWL?" someone questioned.

"SINK BOWL!" answered someone else.

"SINKHOLE!" exclaimed Mr. Spann. "What sinkhole? I know of no sinkhole." He hollered back, "What are you talkin' 'bout?"

"Come on over!" Pete coaxed. "See for yo'self!"

Mr. Spann put a foot forward, then caught hisself, and smiled. Pete could see his smile, and knew that he'd be hard to convince. So he began his spiel.

"Yeah, back durin' the War of 1812 they was inspectin' all the coastal forts and ferries and bridges," Pete reported. "My grand-daddy was an official coast watcher 'round here then, and an engineer, to boot. He told me they found a big sinkhole on this side of the bridge. It was bound to come back."

"Impossible!" Mr. Spann shouted. "You're lyin', you rascal! I ought to come over there and—"

"Do what? Bore me with your alleged engineerin' expertise? This here's a sinkhole big enough to swallow a horse, and it'll only get bigger."

"There is no sinkhole!" Mr. Spann declared.

"How would you know?" retorted Pete. "You was workin' in the dark, and you built right into the pluff mud! What were you thinkin'? No, I mean, *what,* were you thinkin'?" With that, Pete put his thumb to his nose, spread out his fingers and wiggled 'em, to cock a snook at the Devil hisself.

That did it. Pete did expect Mr. Spann to be upset, but he didn't know how the Devil would come at him. Then he did, in an instant. It was barely the blink of an eye, when the Devil dashed across the bridge, leavin' along behind him a red-tinted vapor trail hangin' the length of the span.

"Show me this stinkin' sinkhole!" demanded the Devil, bellowin' into Pete's sunburned face.

"Hole?" Pete looked perplexed. "What hole? Looks to me like the whole thing has been, well, built over."

The Devil was stopped in his tracks. A low, smolderin' fury was risin' in him. His eyes glowed red.

"Speakin' of buildin' over," continued Pete. "We have a contract, signed, sealed, and now delivered, concernin' this very bridge, do we not?"

"You mean this?" snarled the Devil, pullin' out the document from the day before.

"Yes," Pete remarked. "'Specially the part, 'Whereas, the first person to cross the newly repaired Ashley Ribbah Bridge, shall forthwith pay forfeit with his or her mortal soul.' I'd say you qualify, one way or another."

"But I'm the Devil!"

"Consider this a homecomin', of sorts."

"But I rebuilt this bridge for your own good!"

"Sometimes the good ya do don't do ya no good, y'know?" Pete reminded him.

"Well, here, maybe this will do you and me both some good," said the Devil.

He swung his leg back and then forwards in a half-circle arc, aimin' to kick Pete into neighborin' Dorchester County, but Pete simply stepped aside. Hittin' nothin', the Devil instead swept hisself off his other foot, with the bonus of his boot becomin' airborne in the follow-through. That was the ha-ha-funny thing. The odd-funny thing was the bared foot, or rather, the naked hoof of a goat that was thusly revealed by this action. To add insult to the insult, the Devil landed on his rump, in the—yeah, in the pluff mud.

"So, our bridge will stay, and I'll be okay," quipped Pete.

"The deuce, you say!" screamed the Devil. He jumped up, stamped his hoof-foot, twirled his cane, snapped his long fingers, and disappeared in a flash of white light. The telltale smell of sulfur hung across the space where the Devil, Mr. Spann, had stood.

Pete gave the "okay" signal to the townsfolk, who okayed back with a cheer for the new bridge. Then Pete picked up the Devil's kicked-off boot, and boldly stepped across the newly rebuilt Ashley Ribbah Bridge. When he put his foot down on the city side, nothin' happened to him. Again, the townsfolk cheered.

No one could criticize the risky hand played by Pete. His practical freemasonry over the bridge was outstandin'. Pete was a bona fide hero. Yet the Yankees never did find out how the bridge got fixed. Nobody knows the whereabouts of the Devil's boot, either—could be that's where we get the expression "Hell for leather."

Well-suh, that there's the story of the "wreck-construction" of the Ashley Ribbah Bridge. As long as they is a story to tell, someone to tell it, and somebodies to tell it to, such stories as this one will live on, too. That's the fact of the matter.

Speakin' of facts, were you here for Hurricane Hugo, back in 1989? Remember the Ben Sawyer Bridge, that connects Sullivan's Island to the mainland at Mt. Pleasant—the cantilevered bridge batted all cater-wonk? That was one banjaxed bridge, but we fixed it quick. Could that have been the Devil tryin' to get back at us by cockin' a snook at Chawl-stin?

Who knows? But y'all should always beware, 'cause Ol'

Scratch is always tryin' to mess things up for us all. Be thankful for the newest Cuppah Ribbah Bridge, and all the other bridges across Chawl-stin. Bridges connect us all, like a good story.

I just nodded my head, and said, "Jim, I believe you have constructed a whole tale out of pluff mud. I don't mean the story stinks—no, it has a satisfying aroma all its own."

Reflections on Relations

Jim was reminded of this story during the autumn anniversary of the classic football match between the University of South Carolina and Clemson University. The winner gets braggin' rights until next year. The way Jim sees it, regardless of the score, everyone in Carolina wins.

They was a time, long ago when folks were first settlin' in Carolina, and lived away up in the upstate, pretty good and far from what anyone today or then would call civilization. Folks up in the wilderness didn't have a lot of the life-accomodatin' things that folks livin' in the coastal port of Chawl-stin could get. Frenstance, folks back up in the woods had never seen such a common-day thing as a mirror.

One day, a fella by the name of Clem, who lived not far from where North and South Carolina and Georgia meet, decided to travel down to Chawl-stin to barter with the merchants for some household goods. For his wife and his mama he got some sweet-grass baskets, some homegrown tea, and bolts of indigo cloth. For his daddy he got some smoke-cured ham and some pork-cured tobacco, and for his son, Clem got a brand-new pocket knife.

He was still browsin' the market, goin' from stall to stall to see all the wares, when he saw a small, strange, round, flat, shiny

59

thing. Clem looked at it, and a man's face looked back at him. Clem smiled, and the man smiled back at him. Clem stuck out his tongue, and the man stuck out his tongue. Clem was fascinated by this magic man, so he bought the little hand mirror.

All the way home, Clem kept lookin' at the magic man and chucklin' over his funny faces. Clem decided that this was his gift for this trip, since everyone else in the family would be gettin' somethin' special. Besides, the magic might wear off. So Clem decided he'd keep it to hisself.

At home, Clem hid the mirror in a trunk at the foot of his bed. Every once in a while Clem would take it out secretly, laugh with sheer joy, and then hide it again. It was his own amusement.

His wife noticed that Clem would disappear from time to time, so she began to watch him, thinkin' maybe he had a jar of 'shine hidden. She'd hear him laughin' and wondered, "Why is he laughin' when they ain't nothin' to laugh at?"

One mornin', peekin' through the bedroom window, she saw him take a small, strange, round, flat, shiny thing out of the trunk, look into it, and smile. It wasn't just a grin—it was a mile-wide smile. When he went out again, she went into the bedroom, dug out the mirror and glanced at it.

"Oh, oh!" she cried. "Why that unfaithful cheat!" She ran to her mother-in-law, with the mirror in her hand, just a-wailin'. "My faithless husband, your son, didn't want to show the rest of us what he brung home for hisself, and now I know why. He brought hisself a pretty young woman from Chawl-stin, he did, and he keeps her locked in a trunk at the foot of our bed!"

"I don't believe it," her mother-in-law said. "Clem's a good son. He'd never do the like."

"Well, look at her! There she is!" cried the wife as she handed the mirror to her mother-in-law.

"Oh, stop your wailin'," Clem's wife's mother-in-law (that is, Clem's mama) said. "Let me see this young beauty you're ravin' about." She glanced into the mirror, and burst out laughin'. "Ho, ho, ho! My son might not be the sharpest knife in the drawer, but why in the world would he prefer to bring home such a wrinkled old hag as this is beyond me. You're foolish to be so jealous!"

Right about then, Clem's wife's mother-in-law's husband (that is, Clem's daddy) walked past the doorway and stopped to wonder why his wife was laughin' and his daughter-in-law was cryin'. They explained the problem to him, and he just scowled.

"Let me see for myself," he declared. He took the mirror and looked into it. Then he looked back at the women, shruggin' his shoulders and rollin' his eyes. "You silly women," he said. "This ain't no female, young or old. I don't see how y'all could mistake it. This here's our neighbor's grandpa. You can plainly see his shiny bald head and his scraggly old goat's beard!"

Well, they kept takin' turns lookin' and lookin' into the mirror. The wife kept seein' a pretty young woman. Her mother-in-law kept seein' a wrinkled old hag. Her father-in-law kept seein' the neighbor's dodderin' old grandpa. Not a one of 'em could convince the others about what they each saw. The mirror got tossed onto the bed durin' the argument.

That's when Clem's wife's mother-in-law's husband's grandson (that is, Clem's son) strolled by, wonderin' what the grown-ups were arguin' about. He knew better than to interrupt they conversation, lively as it was, so he pulled out his new pocket knife and looked 'round for somethin' to whittle. The only thing that caught his eye was the small, strange, round, flat, shiny thing on the bed. "Let me see," he said as he picked it up.

What he saw was a young boy holdin' a brand new knife just like his. "Well, I'll be!" he cried. "How the devil did you get a-hold of my new knife?"

When he got no answer, he shouted, "You better give me back my knife!"

But all he saw was a scowlin', pinch-faced little boy, still holdin' his knife.

"Ma!" he screamed. "Pa! Pa, come git my knife back from this brat!"

Well, Clem's wife's mother-in-law's husband's grandson's daddy (that is, Clem hisself) came a-runnin', and burst into the bedroom full of fitful, fumin', frustrated, family members.

"Whatever is the matter, son?" he asked.

"He stole my new knife, and he won't give it back!" whined his son.

"Let me see here," said Clem, and he took the mirror from his son. Clem was already upset, so when he gazed into the mirror all he saw was an angry, frownin' man. "It's you!" he cried. "I should have known. It was all too good to be true. Why, you skunk! I brung you all the way from Chawl-stin back here to my home, only to find out you ain't nothin' but a common thief! I know just how to fix you, mister!"

And with that, Clem ran out the house and down to the creek. The whole family followed him. Then he said, "You've been caught thievin' red-handed, mister." The magic man just frowned at Clem. "And I don't have a rope long enough to hang you." The magic man scowled at Clem. "But I got the next-best thing, so I'm gonna drown you!" And Clem bared his teeth at the man, but he just grimaced back at Clem. "Enough of you!" Clem shouted as he flung the mirror into the creek. It sank without a trace.

That was the end of the thievin' magic man, and the pretty young woman, and the wrinkled old hag, and the neighbor's gnarled grandpa, and the whinin' brat who looked back at each of 'em from the small, strange, round, flat, shiny thing. Ever after that Clem and his family refused to make any more reflections on they relations.

"If you're wonderin' how it is that I happen to know about all of these historic, histrionic happenin's, so as to tell 'em to you," Jim explained, "this story has been handed down through all of Clem's sons, till one of 'em told it to me, and now I've told it to you."

"After all, Jim," I reminded him, "you can't keep a good story to yourself!"

The Luck of the Irish Fella

My friend, Jim Aisle, locally known as The Lowcountry Liar, told me at a St. Patrick's Day celebration, "This tale grew out of the era known as Reconstruction, or as some of us here in Chawl-stin refer to it, the era of 'Wreck-Construction.'"

They was a man and his wife with no children, but instead, the man's ma and pa lived with 'em on the old family homestead. What they was left of it, anyway. What had started out as a king's grant of three hundred acres for hearth and home a century ago had become a post-war mandate one-tenth that size. Most of that forfeit land was too tore up to farm anythin' worth anythin' for a while, anyhow.

Well-suh, this fella was a man of small luck, but his wife was lovin', and his parents had they health. At least they had until early 1865, when his ma was blinded by the flash of a Yankee bomb blast. In this un-Civil War, Southern civilians sometimes were not spared the sword, even if it only seemed like the flat of the blade. By then, this fella and his pa, who were servin' the South, had had they fill of fightin'—and then suddenly, the war was over, so they came home.

The Union Army now occupied the Lowcountry, and, allied

with Northern carpetbaggers and Southern scalawags, they made everyday goods and services good and scarce. Food was nearly nonexistent. The fella—I don't know if I know his right name, but he was a big, friendly, red-headed Irish fella—I maybe recollect the last name of McCann.

Anyway, this fella McCann and his pa worked what little plot of land they had left, with his wife and his ma workin' alongside 'em. Despite all of they hard work, everythin' they did was still not enough to sustain theyselves, and certainly none of the nearby strangers would have any sympathy should they starve. That was not a solution.

Now, by an arrangement among the authorities, they was keepin' all of Johns and Wadmalaw Islands off-limits to everyone but the Army in order to have a game preserve from which to pluck provisions. Anyone, be they black, white, or Southern, would be shot on sight for poachin'. If the poacher should stand trial, the scales of Justice would swing in balance over the high limb of a nearby oak tree.

This fella McCann could only hazard his hide against a certain, slow, shrinkin' demise. Whatever the risk, he was determined to feed his family, so he was gonna find a way in and out of that game preserve. He was game for the game of the game, you might say. Well, okay, you might not.

Anyway, he set off in a borrowed rowbo-it, and, slippin' past the pickets, made his way along the Stono Ribbah. He finally found a secluded, quiet cove on the western shore of Johns Island. There he secured the boat, and stepped into the woods.

All he had to hunt with was a kitchen knife, a length of rope, and a croker sack. All he saw were some rabbits and squirrels that scampered away out of sight or out of reach. All day long he searched for somethin' to save his starvin' family, but it seemed all the animals stayed hidden, and the birds in the branches above seemed to mock his earnest efforts.

Then he spotted the deer. It was a white-tail buck—but wait! No, it was an all-white deer—snow white from tail to nose tip, and down to its hooves. Never had McCann seen such a sight.

The deer looked at him, but did not bolt. McCann carefully approached the animal, while stealthily unsheathin' the knife from the burlap bag. He neared the deer, which did not twitch, and as he steadied hisself just before strikin', the deer spoke:

"Good man, McCann. Hold down your hand!

Hear me now, and, you'll understand.

Do not slay me, or the Yankees

Will hang you for me, from a high oak tree.

If you will spare my life,

You, your folks, and your wife,

May be saved from starvation.

I can be your salvation."

McCann couldn't believe his ears. This deer wasn't from 'round here, was it? A white deer, that speaks, and in rhyme? He thought his hunger was makin' him hallucinate. Then the deer spoke again.

"If you spare me, I guarantee

One wish for you. What do you choose?"

He was speechless. A magical, all-white, rhyme-speakin', wish-givin' deer was offerin' him a possible solution to his dire problem. Could he refuse? What should he wish for, with only one wish? What if this was a ruse? Would the family be satisfied?

Finally he said, "All right," but he didn't know if it was right. "You can go," he added, but he wasn't sure that it would work. "But I'll meet you here tomorrow!" he called out. The white deer bowed its head once, and instead of runnin' off, followed him back to his bo-it, and watched him row away.

He made his way home safely again, and as he came down the road, saw his pa toilin' in the field. He couldn't relate what he thought he saw in the woods, it was too outlandish. He decided to take another tack.

"Hey, pa," he said, "have you ever thought what you would wish for if you only had the one wish?"

"Hah! That's an easy one," said his pa. "Gold, son, I'd wish for gold. Up to at least your own weight in gold. Foldin' money ain't worth its paper these days, Confederate or Federal. Gold will last, and pay your way all your days, son. Yessuh, I'd surely wish for gold!"

That was definitely a worthy reply. Still, money doesn't solve every problem; if it did, it would grow on trees. He saw his ma sittin' on the stoop shellin' peas, so he went to ask her opinion.

"Ma," he said, "if you had just the one wish, what would you wish for?"

"Oh, darlin', I don't know," she said with a sigh. "Not to be selfish, now, but I do believe I would have to ask for my eyesight back. I miss your sweet face, son, and I miss the beautiful Carolina sunsets."

"No, mama," he assured her. "You're not ever in the least bit selfish."

Still and all, he would have to hear what his wife had to say. Seems a married man has to check with his better half, at least half of the time. She was inside the house, sewin' a patch on a patched-up pair of pants.

"Sugar," he said, "tell me, if you were ever granted a single, solitary wish, not three like in fairy tales, but only the one wish, what is it you would wish to have?"

She put down her work, to contemplate. After a moment she told him. "Honey, if wishes could come true, even in these bad times, I'd still wish for this. We've been married for the length of the war, and we haven't had a chance to start, let alone raise, a family, but I want children. I know how hard things are now, but children bring you joy with they laughter, they keep you young, and they are the future. Children, love, is what I'd wish for."

He had heard from all parties they particular wishes, and which was the better, he couldn't tell. Besides, he hadn't decided a wish for hisself. How would he choose?

All night long he tossed in bed, turnin' over in his mind the many options. All of his energy was put into weighin' and counter-weighin' each request. All he had was the hope that he would do the right thing, and his family would survive.

Come the mornin', he knew what he would choose. He kissed his wife, hugged his ma, shook hands with his pa, and set off again for the game preserve on Johns Island. He bypassed the pickets again, and safely snuck along the Stono, till he came 'round to the shaded cove once more. There on the shore stood the white deer.

McCann moored the bo-it, then moved to the deer. The animal was as brilliantly white as before, a stunnin' sight. It looked at him with its large, dark eyes.

"Well," said McCann, "here we are again. I wasn't sure this was real, but I can see sure, it is. Gotta have faith, I guess. Well, I don't know what power you possess, but I believe you, nonetheless."

"That is very good to hear, for my magic is sincere," said the deer.

"I've decided on that one wish you said you'd grant me. I talked it over with the members of my family, to see what they all thought. I love 'em deeply, each and every one, but I finally have to make this decision."

"Whatever you decide, by that I shall abide," replied the deer. "I shall now grant your one wish, then you and I are finished."

"Fair enough," said McCann. "This is the wish I ask you to grant me, now: I wish that my mother could see her grandchildren eatin' off of plates of gold!"

"Jim," I said to him, "you must have a chip of the Blarney Stone in one of your fillings!"

Deep in the Heart of It

Jim recounted to me, during our general flow of discussion in which I made mention of the stereotypical Wild West Cowboy, that he had met one, right here, in downtown Charleston, once upon a time.

Yeah, back when I was engaged as a student at our municipal namesake's "College of Knowledge," I was also employed pullin' taps at a hole-in-the-wall down at the corner of Wentworth and St. Philip, called the Hog Penny. Late one Friday afternoon, before the last class transcended to the first glass and the weekend crowds filled up the place, one of your stereotypical Texas-sized All-American, ten gallon hat, chaps, boots, and spurs, cactus-straight, Clint Eastwood-squint, Randolph Scott of a cowboy came in and ordered a beer.

I pulled him a draft, he paid his coin, and he saluted the room with his chin. Everyone was watchin' the cowboy drinkin' his beer, when I noticed a coupla frat boys look out the window, then leave real easy-like out the front door. They slipped back in as the cowboy finished his beer. He set down his mug, nodded a thanks, turned and walked out the door. I could see him standin' out there on the sidewalk, hands on his hips, lookin' up and down the street like he missed somethin'. He came back in the

Hog Penny and stood blockin' the entrance to announce, "Folks, could I have your undivided attention, please! Now, I'm not from 'round these parts, I'm just passin' through. I came in here to wet my whistle, and I tied up my mount right outside this front door. While I had a beer some low-down, no-account, coyote-kissin' varmint stole my horse!"

Nobody moved in that room. It was a Hollywood-Kodak moment. Then he said, "Now, I'm gonna have me another beer. When I'm done, I'll leave. But my horse, saddle, bridle, and all had better be back, tied up like I left it. Otherwise, I'll have to do what I done in Tulsa when some snake stole my horse. I didn't like what I had to do there and then, 'twern't nice and 'twern't purty. So now, I'm gonna have another beer."

Well, I pulled him another draft, he paid again and drank slowly, puttin' all his concentration on the precious fortifyin' carbonized beverage before him. I watched those same frat boys quickly down they drinks and, less easily, leave the premises. They didn't return, neither. The cowboy drained his mug, placed it on the bar, turned to scan the room, then walked to the door, and saw his horse hitched to a parkin' meter two steps away. He glanced over his shoulder at the rest of us, touched the brim of his Stetson, and stepped across the threshold.

"Hey, wait a minute!" I shouted at him. He stopped and turned in the doorway. "What was it, mister, that you had to do in Tulsa that time when someone stole your horse?"

"Hmmm. Well, I'll tell you, since you asked. 'Twern't purty and 'twern't nice, and it made me right uncomfortable to have to do it. When they stole my horse, I had to walk home."

He stared at me like Gary Cooper, then mounted his horse and rode off, westward, naturally. Y'know, where the deer and the antelope play?

Jim smiled his storyteller smile. I had to admit that if seldom is heard a discouraging word from Jim, it still sounds absurd.

Dixie's Lowcountry Roots

One time when I drove down to Beaufort on some business, my story-teller friend Jim Aisle rode shotgun and fired off one story after another. At some point I noticed the weather of the day and made mention of the relative humidity. Jim expanded on my statement with this ghostly story.

Some folks say the South has an air all its own. Maybe it results from the stewed union of nearly ceaseless sunshine, the seasonal heat of the latitude, the incessant humidity. Or, as is said down in the Lowcountry: "It ain't the heat that'll get ya, it's the humility!" 'Low me to 'splain.

On any given day under the Carolina blue sky from Chawl-stin to Hilton Head, sundry numbers of tourists swell the steady stream of traffic on U.S. Highway 17. Along this artery, about halfway 'tween the Ashepoo and Combahee Ribbahs in the environs of Green Pond, lies a junction with State Route 303 and a dirt road. The dirt road is an extended driveway to the humble country homes in the neighborhood.

Standin' like a sentry at the junction is a well-weathered general store, the likes of which is often depicted in paintin's of the quiet, rural South. The store stands—almost squats—on its cinderblock legs, as solid and silent as the surroundin' gray oaks hangin' with grayer Spanish moss. Wherever they is shade 'round the store they is an ever-changin' encampment of mostly young black men, the ever-present local citizens ever-ready to bear witness to the passin' of humanity.

Such a settin' may seem serene, but a sense of forebodin' surrounds the site like an unseen shroud. Maybe it's superstition and has somethin' to do with numerology. Frenstance, with the highways, the number 17 itself is prime, and the 7 in 17 is deemed lucky. However, 303 has three digits that added together equal six, and three sixes is a sure sign of somethin' seriously sinister.

· · ·

Every year durin' spring break time, hordes of holiday highway traffic head south for Florida rendezvous in Daytona Beach, Orlando, and Fort Lauderdale. Vehicles of motley makes with license plates from every state flash by full of native Southerners, "damned Yankees," and other curious foreigners on tour, all just passin' through. The constant crowd by the general store languidly watches the motorists like an alligator awaitin' lunch.

An old savvy huntin' dog, a bluetick coonhound, half hibernatin' under the store porch, rouses itself from the well-worn groove of its crawl space berth, pokes its nose into the midday sunshine. Slow as a turtle, the hound dog exposes itself bit by bit from under the porch, and barks hoarsely when all but its tail is sunlit. A few in the crowd look at the old country canine, then at each other, then back at the traffic.

Three teenagers—one tall and lanky, one short and round, one big and beefy as a football player—arise from the shade, shuffle toward the tarmac as the hound, tail a-waggin', moves to follow 'em. A soft jinglin' sound emanates from the anklets the teens wear, silver rings strung with shiny dimes to ward off evil. Instead of a dog collar, the hound wears a similar dime ring.

They wait by the edge of the road, as patient as pallbearers, timin' the passin' cars for as much space on the southbound lane as on the northbound. Then, quick as a switch is thrown, they dash across the highway, the hound at they heels, barkin' in triumph as they all cross safely. The teens chuckle and smile.

"Whacha say there, Dixie?" one of 'em calls to the dog.

They walk single file up Route 303, the dog Dixie followin', trottin' alongside, runnin' ahead to stop for the trio to catch up, then repeatin' the onward dance. For such a seemin'ly old dog, Dixie steps lightly in an almost fluid movement. About half a mile from the intersection Dixie halts, bays like a bugler, and the teens turn off down a path into the pines, disappearin' from view of the general store one by one. Before long, a pungent, sweet smoke emanates from they general direction.

· · ·

A half hour later the teens emerge with bleary eyes, silly smiles, and loud talk. Dixie steps 'round 'em carefully, deliberately, and follows 'em back to the intersection. They all wait again, timin' the traffic spacin'. Without hurry they finally cross durin' a lull of the passersby.

Dixie starts across, but stops at the center line and turns back, retreatin' off the road. Then goin' into a wind-up, makin' three small circles counterclockwise, Dixie again starts across the southbound lane. By then, a red Jeep Cherokee with Vermont tags has appeared.

The brakes scream, the horn shouts—*thump, crunch!*—a sharp, short yelp from Dixie, and it's all over before it's all realized.

The Jeep swerves off the road, skids across the gravel shoulder, and stops yards from the impact. The spectators 'round the general store stop as if in freeze-frame. The three teens rush back to the road. The northbound traffic slows down to gawk; the southbound traffic stops.

Surveyin' the scene some cry out for poor Dixie, some approach the driver, who is shaken up but unhurt. Two other riders bail out of the Jeep. They look like typical college frat boys on spring break. Everyone seems okay. There is no noticeable damage to the bumper, or the grill, or any of the front end of the Jeep.

"My God! My God! Oh, my God!" wails the driver. "I didn't even see it! The dog just darted out in front of me. I couldn't stop . . . I couldn't stop."

His companions comfort him. They try not to look at Dixie. They ain't much to see: an old, dead, bluetick coonhound lookin' more like a crumpled cardboard box by the side of a usually sleepy Southern road.

The body is twisted 'round and folded on itself, both head and tail pointin' southwest. The spine is broken at the neck and hips, the legs all twisted akimbo. They's no blood, which looks worse somehow. They is an awkward silence as everyone assesses the situation, before any authoritative decisions are made.

The three teenagers make they way through the gaggle of onlookers to the three travelers. The teenagers ain't angry, although they dog is dead. It was an accident surely, yet a loss has occurred. Retribution is not the issue, compensation is.

"Hey, man, that was our dog you hit," the tall teen says flatly.

"Ohhh, God. I am so sorry, so sorry," answers the driver. "I couldn't stop, I swear. What could I do?"

"Looked like it changed its mind or whatever, y'know?" says his friend.

"I bet it was a good dog, though," offers the other.

"Yeah, Dixie's some kind of dog, all right," replies the tall teen, "Or was."

"And you could say she has, uh, had, a mind all her own," adds the short teen. The beefy teen smiles a toothy grin.

"How can I ever make this up to you?" asks the driver.

They's a soberin' silence from the three teens, who glance at each other knowin'ly. The driver and his companions—college kids wearin' the same fraternity T-shirts that announce, "The University of Vermont—in the Land of the Green Mountains!"—look at each other without a clue about what to do.

"Well, Dixie was a good coonhound," the tall teen explains, "and she could hold her own with any huntin' dog in the whole Lowcountry. We've had her for over twenty years, so she—"

"Was valuable," says the short teen.

"Yeah, real valuable," says the beefy teen.

"And you can't really measure your feelin's for a friend like Dixie," adds the tall teen. He leaves the sentiment hangin' in the air like Spanish moss.

The three college kids nod they heads in assent. They shoulders sag with an unseen weight. Everyone knows that feelin' of loss: what had been or could be, but will not be any more. Somethin' taken with no questions asked.

"Say, would you excuse me and my friends a minute?" the driver asks.

"Sure."

Steppin' back to the Jeep, the college kids talk among theyselves, each in turn a-lookin' up at the three teens, at Dixie, at the gathered crowd. They each reach into they back pockets for they wallets. Between 'em they pull out bills in double digits, the driver the most. With a loud sigh, he folds the money into he palm, walks back to the teens.

"I . . . I don't know how to make this up to you, except with this," he says, offerin' the money. They's easily $200. At first, the teens don't react.

"Hell, man," says the tall teen, "what can I say?" He takes the money, maybe closer to $300, it looks like.

No one speaks. The space between the two groups, like a chasm too wide to bridge, too deep to reach, leaves 'em all standin' there dumbstruck. Finally the teen pockets the money. Then he extends his hand and shakes with the driver, who is wholly relieved.

"No hard feelin's, man," says the teen.

"Yeah, man. No hard feelin's," agrees the driver. "It was an accident, pure and simple, and I'm really, really, really sorry, man."

"It's okay, really," replies the short teen. The beefy teen smiles in agreement.

"I'm glad to hear that," the driver says. "Listen, we've got to get goin', y'know? We're tryin' to get to Florida before nightfall."

"Yeah, sure, we're cool," says the tall teen. "Y'all just watch the road more careful, that's all."

The three college kids take that as they dismissal and walk back to the Jeep. Before they climb in, they reinspect the front for damage, but ain't none apparent. A minute later they merge onto the southbound lane of Highway 17 to rejoin the exodus for Florida.

The two bigger teens stand guard over Dixie's carcass as the short teen hustles to the general store and returns with a light-weight wood crate. Gingerly they pick up Dixie, place her care-fully in the crate. When they can, they quickly cross the highway carryin' the open-air coffin, then start down the dirt road.

The usual curious crowd re-forms 'round the store for a sat-isfyin' discussion of the incident, and turn it into an event, a memory. As the teens pass, no one speaks, a few heads nod, oth-ers only stare. The teens don't say nothin' as they carry the remains of they best friend past the store, down the long straight stretch of the dirt road, and out of sight 'round a bend.

• • •

After about a mile from the bend, the teens step into the woods, make they way to a huge magnolia tree beside a slow-movin' creek. Part of the bank has eroded to create a kind of cove with a dark, quiet pool beneath some exposed roots of the magnolia tree. The teens put down they burden, clamber down the bank, and, stoopin' below the twisted roots, walk 'round the pool.

Wedged between the roots, snugly tucked under a tarp, lies a padlocked plastic chest. They haul the chest and tarp up to the crate, and take a moment to catch a breath. Then without a word, they begin a solemn business by unfoldin' the tarp and unlockin' the chest.

Out of the chest they take a quilt that they spread over the tarp. They pull out the other contents: a half-gallon can of tur-pentine, three trim-work paint brushes, a half-quart Pyrex mea-surin' cup, a metal teakettle, a half pint of Wild Turkey, a fat red candle, some linen cloth, a spool of string, and a pair of scissors. At the bottom of the chest is a tray arrayed with a variety of vials filled with herbal remedies. Out of the tray they select green cock-lebur, cherry root, oak bark, dogwood root, cassena leaf from the Sea Island shrub, gunpowder, buzzard grease, desiccated earth-worm, and two little bottles of graveyard dirt—goofer dust—taken from the graves of both a devout, evangelizin' Christian and an unrepentant, convicted criminal.

The short teen takes the teakettle to fetch some water from the pool, while the other two unbox Dixie and lay her out on the quilt. They break up the crate and make a cook fire. Takin' the turpentine, they fill the measurin' cup up to the midline, pour in half as much still water, add a bit of green cocklebur and earthworm, a pinch of gunpowder, a jigger of whiskey, and three drops of candle wax. They hold the cup over the fire just long enough to heat the mix through.

Dippin' the paintbrushes into it they coat Dixie's body with the elixir—a folk-honored, time-proven antibiotic balm that erases the abrasions from the hound's hide. They rub in buzzard grease, which works like WD-40 to limber up the leg joints, hips, neck, spine. The body has not stiffened at all, but is like a jelly-filled bagpipe that the teens handle easily like old pros.

"Don't look like she'll need a poultice," the tall teen remarks.

"Nah, they didn't even break the skin this time," observes the short teen.

"I think the guy was tryin' to avoid Dixie," the big teen says.

"They always do," replies the short teen.

They all smile, then laugh together. A little more inspection, a few dabs here and there, and they are satisfied with the work. They rinse the brushes and cup in the creek.

They bring back a measure of the runnin' creek water to make a tea of cherry and dogwood root, oak bark, and cassena leaf. While the water heats in the kettle, they make a teabag with some linen, pack it with the ingredients and tie it with string. When the water is ready, they again fill the measurin' cup halfway and drop in the teabag. The beneficial properties of the ingredients seep into the brackish water, givin' it a red tint. While they wait for the tea to cool, the teens roll up some other herbal "tea" in cigarette papers, and soon again the pungent, sweet smoke is curlin' through the air.

• • •

"Ready for the dust?" asks the tall teen, awhile later.

The other two nod. With the knife they cut a square of linen and a long length of string. Onto the square they shake a few grains of the good and the bad goofer dust, then add three hairs pulled from Dixie's tail. They put the patch of dusty linen over her nose and tie it to the back of her head.

The tea is tepid, ready to drink. The two bigger teens hold Dixie, nose to the sky, keepin' the patch in place, as the short teen slowly pours the tea down her throat. Not a drop is wasted. As the potion goes down they intone:

"Bring me back from Beyond—Go! Bring me back from
    Below!
My time's not done, my soul's unsung,
Now bring me back from Beyond!
Paint nine parts Protector, Drink six Fortifier, Breathe three
    Unifier!
Add equal parts from both good and bad,
Plus three old parts from the life you had,
Now bring me back from Beyond!"

In unison the teens say, "amen," then lay Dixie down again on the quilt, and step back. They wait and watch for an affect, a change. Then, a shudder . . . another . . . a stir, a jerk . . . eyelids half-raise, then close . . . then nothin'. Not a twitch.

A moment later, a sharp spasm stiffens the spine, sticks the legs straight out and the tail straight up. The eyes of Dixie open wide and stare up at the teens. Her tail beats the quilt, *whump, whump, whump.*

"She's b-a-a-a-ck!" the short teen announces like an emcee. "Presto, change-o!" They all laugh.

Dixie lifts her head and sneezes. They help her sit up, take the patch off her nose, and pat her affectionately. She licks they hands and faces, the silver dime necklace jinglin' merrily.

• • •

While Dixie rests in the shade of the magnolia, a-pantin' happily, the teens clean up. The quilt is refolded and tamped down into the chest, the chest is locked again, and the tarp is gathered. Back down the bank and under the tree they carry the chest, resettle it among the roots, and cover it with the tarp.

They wash up at the creek and climb back up to Dixie and what's left of the fire. The short teen pulls out a small onion from his pocket and tosses it to his big friend on his left. The big teen stabs a long thumbnail into the onion, cuts a ring out of the layers, and passes the onion to the tall teen at his left. In turn they cut out rings and drop 'em into the final flames, a sealant on they friendship.

As an acrid aroma arises from the fire, the tall teen pulls out the wad of bills, starts countin'. His lips purse, brows furrow, eyes grow wide as the number rises. At last, he slaps the wad against he palm.

"Oooo-eeee! Thuh-ree hundred and for-tee dollars for the afternoon, gentlemen!" he claims. The other teens shake they heads, a-grinnin'.

"Guess I'll put some of my share toward my college fund!" boasts the short teen. They all laugh again.

The big teen asks, "What's our shares, after tithin'?"

"Let's see," says the tall teen, "that be thirty-four dollars for the graves. That leaves us, uh, what?"

"About three-oh-six," the short teen says proudly.

"Hmmm, that be a hundred and two dollars apiece," states the big teen.

"My man, Mister Math," jokes the tall teen.

He pulls from his pockets two more rolls of money, shuffles some bills, makin' change. Then he doles out they shares. They each re-count, and when sure of they tallies, stuff the money into they pockets. At the last, the tithe money is added to the smallest roll.

"Count that," says the short teen. "I want to know what today's take is."

"Oh, man, Mister Accountant," the tall teen comments, rollin' his eyes. "Don't worry. The spirits'll get they fair share. It'll be right."

"Or it wouldn't be quality dust," agrees the big teen.

"Well, count it anyway," the short teen replies. "I like knowin' the score."

"All right, all right."

Slow and steady, so as not to miss a single bill, the teens count out the overhead expense of they operation.

" . . . ninety-one, ninety-two, ninety-three, ninety-four," says the tall teen. "That's ninety-four dollars for goofer dust."

"That's nine hundred forty dollars for the day!" exclaims the short teen.

"So far," the big teen adds.

"Think Dixie's up to one more today?" asks the tall teen.

"Let's get supper first," the short teen says, "I'm hongry."

"Yeah, me too," nods the big teen.

"All right," says the tall teen. He calls, "C'mon, Dixie! Let's go!"

Dixie jumps up, tail a-waggin', ready for sport. The teens knock down and stomp out the fire. A last look 'round, then they all head back to the highway.

• • •

Most maps of the Carolina Lowcountry that any tourist might mark up with points of interest and alternate routes will not show any sign that a certain point on U.S. Highway 17 South has any particular importance. However, some other visitors no doubt have red lines, yellow highlights, star asterisks, or large block letters earmarkin' the very spot where they accidentally hit and killed a dog—an old, bluetick coonhound, in fact—and paid a price, literally, that put a dent in they wallets and in they pride. As the sayin' goes among the neighborly folks down 'round Green Pond, 'tween the Ashepoo and the Combahee, "It ain't the heat that'll get ya, it's the humility!"

I sighed and said to Jim, "After all, it's a living."

Jack and the Dancin' Palmetto Bugs

Most folks agree that the unofficial state pest of South Carolina—if not the entire South—is the notorious cockroach, or palmetto bug. According to my storyteller friend Jim Aisle, known locally as the Lowcountry Liar, even this lowly life has a good side. This is what he told me.

Just as typical as an old joke, they once was a widow and her only son, named Jack, and together they owned one cow. They lived near Chawl-stin, west of the Ashley Ribbah, happy and well enough for a good while, but finally tough times came and only got tougher. The crops failed, the plumbin' went out, the rent went up, and poverty looked to move in next door. Things got rubbed so thin for the poor widow and Jack that for want of money and bare necessities, they decided to sell the cow.

"Jack," says his mama to him one night, "go over in the mornin' to the market downtown and sell the cow. Be careful, son, don't let no one cheat you. Get good value for the trade."

"Yes, ma'am," says Jack, "I'll make the best of all trades."

Good 'nuff. In the mornin' brave Jack gets up early, takes his walkin' stick in hand to turn out the cow, and off to the Chawl-stin market he goes with her. When Jack nears the market, he sees a great crowd gathered in the street, so he tethers the cow and goes into the crowd to see what everyone is lookin' at.

There in the middle of 'em all he sees a li'l white-whiskered man wearin' a red ball cap. He has in one hand a mouse with a teeny tiny tweezers it holds to its mouth. In the li'l man's other hand stands a pair of palmetto bugs, apparently wearin' some sort of red and yellow apparel.

When the li'l man puts 'em down on the ground, claps his hands twice and whistles, the mouse begins to pluck the tweez-ers, makin' a strange hummin' sound. The two palmetto bugs stand up on they hind legs, take a-hold of each other here 'n' there 'n' here 'n' there and begin dancin'. As soon as they start up, they's not a man nor woman, nor anythin' at the market, that don't set to dancin', too.

In the street the horse carriages rock and roll as the horses dance on they hind legs, and the wheels on the carts whirl 'round on they own. In the nearby restaurants, the kitchen pots and pans clang together as the diners and the staff jump up to jitterbug. Someone plays the spoons, too. Everyone is jumpin' and jiggin' and reelin', includin' Jack and his cow. The Chawl-stin market has never before nor since been in such a state of sheer excite-ment.

After a while, the li'l white-whiskered man pulls the bill of his red ball cap, whistles, and claps his hands twice again to make the music stop. Then the li'l man picks up the tweezers-pluckin' mouse and the two dandy palmetto bugs, and puts 'em into his coat pocket. The men, women, pots and pans, Jack, his cow, and all else come to a sudden stop. Instantly, everyone breaks down in such laughter that could break your heart for bein' lifted to such heights of joy.

The li'l man turns to Jack and asks, "Jack, how'd ya like the show?"

Jack tells him, "I like it fine. It surely is light-hearted, I'll hand you that."

"Well then, as it lifts your heart and all," says the savvy li'l man, "how would you like to own this menagerie and manage the sideshow?"

"Ooooh, is that possible?" asks Jack with delight.

"Why, sure, anythin' is possible," agrees the li'l man. He tugs at the bill of his cap again, and strokes his whiskers. "What would you say, Jack, to a fair swap and trade of my entertainin' crew for your hapless cow?"

"My mama was hopin' to get value for the sellin' of the cow," Jack explains. "I don't see how—"

"Anyone, even yourself, Jack, couldn't ever pass up such a rare, fantastic, and truly unique opportunity," pitches the li'l man. "It's the chance of a lifetime. The chance of your lifetime, Jack." The li'l man raises his arms and clasps his hands behind his head, then grins and wiggles his bushy eyebrows.

"Well," Jack ruminates, "it is the first time I've ever seen the like, that's for certain. It would likely set mama off on a hearty laughin' fit, fit to be tied, and she surely could use a good laugh these days—"

"She'll laugh like she's never laughed before," adds the li'l man.

"All right, I'll do it!" says Jack.

He strikes the bargain with the li'l man, who happily keeps the cow. Homeward goes brave Jack, with only the mouse and its tweezers, and the pair of palmetto bugs in his pocket. He steps along jauntily, hummin' the new tune, a-twirlin' his walkin' stick like a drum majorette's baton.

"Jack, it's noon, you've come home mighty soon," says his mama when he returns. "I see you don't have the cow. Please, tell me son, you didn't lose the cow instead of sellin' it, now did you?"

"No, Mama, I made a trade, all right."

"That's good, son. Did you get a fair price? And no credit, right?"

"Uh, yes and no."

"What do you mean, Jack?"

"I mean, I got *value*, Mama."

"What kind of a number is that?"

"I don't know, but it must be divisible by three."

Jack pulls from his pocket the palmetto bugs and the mouse. Jack's mama shrieks and rolls her eyes, nearly faintin', but she sits down and holds her head in her hands. Jack sets the trio on the floor, then claps his hands twice and whistles.

The mouse starts pluckin' the tee-tiny tweezers to make the strange hummin' sound. The palmetto bugs rise up to begin dancin'. No sooner do they step up and out, than Jack and his mama have to tap they toes, too. Jack's mama is so taken with the mouse's music and the dandy dancin' that she looks surprised, like from a heart attack, but she lets out a big hearty laugh.

Then the pots and pans 'round the stove start a-clangin' together. The kitchen table and chairs—even the one seatin' Jack's mama—start hoppin' 'round the house with all the other furniture. Pictures hangin' on the walls swing in time to the lively tune.

Before they can slip into a slip jig, Jack gives a whistle, claps his hands twice, and the music stops. As Jack gathers up his group, everythin' else falls back into place. Jack's mama is still laughin', but finally she comes 'round, with only an occasional giggle, like a hiccup.

"Oh, Jack," she says, "that was good for the heart. You're a good-hearted son, and I know you were thinkin' 'nothin's too good for my Mama.' But after all, son, it's really good for nothin'. You sold our one and only cow for this motley crew! Now, what we gonna do?"

She begins to cry. Jack has never seen his mama so upset before. He doesn't know exactly what to do, but he knows he has to do somethin'. It has to be right, and it has to be right quick. So, Jack takes off to think about it. His mama cryin' like that is gettin' him upset, too.

Jack walks along the road contemplatin' till he comes to a bus stop, then sits to rest a minute. A li'l old lady in red tennis shoes is there, too, and she smiles at Jack. Then she nudges him with her foot.

"Why you got such a dry look on you, son?" she asks him.

"Oh, I've ruined my family's future with my foolishness," Jack replies. Then he proceeds to tell her about the li'l white-whiskered man in the red ball cap, the hummin' bein' of the mouse, the dancin' palmetto bugs, everythin'.

"That's heartfelt, for sure," says the li'l woman. "Say, I might know of somethin' that might cheer you up instead."

"What's that?"

"Why, they's a contest goin' on tonight in downtown Chawl-stin, that's fit for fools of all stripes. It's what they call a 'Laugh Contest,' only they've played with the words to call it the 'Laff-on Test.' You could probably enter, maybe even win."

"What's the grand prize?"

"Well, they's money. I don't know that it's a king's ransom, but it'll pay your bills for a while. And they's an all-expenses paid, three-week engagement at some fancy hotel in Las Vegas, where you can do your act, play to the tourists. After that, who knows? With all the attention and endorsements added in, you could be a star."

"It's worth a try. I can't let a chance like this go by."

"Sure thing, but I hear one of the three judges on the panel is a real sourpuss. They say she hasn't laughed so much as three times at anyone in seven years. They call her the princess, 'cause she's kind of prissy and all."

"Well, thanks for the advice. I think I'll just go down and try out. Where it is?"

"Down to the Gaillard Auditorium. It starts at eight, don't be late. Good luck!"

Before Jack heads to town, he runs home to tell his mama what he's up to and for her not to worry. His confidence is reas-surin', and she gets to feelin' better, even fixes him a hearty sup-per before he goes to the show. When he leaves, Jack hides a bis-cuit in his pocket for his pesty performers.

By the time Jack gets to Chawl-stin, makes his way across town, meanders through the large crowd 'round the Gaillard Auditorium, and gets inside to sign up as a contestant, the emcee is introducin' the panel of three judges. First, they's a li'l white-haired gentleman with a full white beard, dressed in a shiny white three-piece suit and a bright red beret. Next, they's a li'l matronly lady, her white hair done up in a high pompadour, a-wearin' a silver sparkly dress and ruby-red high-heel shoes. Finally, they's the so-called princess, a tall, good-lookin' young woman dressed in a golden gown who looks a little sad, 'specially for a laugh contest.

Jack is the last official contestant to enroll, so while he waits to go on, he takes out the mouse and palmetto bugs for inspection. They look none the worse for wear, and half the biscuit is gone, too, he notices. To avoid any backstage accident, Jack unlaces one of his shoes and ties the trio in a line that he can trail behind him. He plans to parade boldly before the panel.

After lots of laughs, the list at last comes down to Jack. He takes a breath, tugs on the shoelace train, and steps from the curtain wing. As he nears center stage and the audience gets a full view of the crew, the tee-hees and chuckles become guffaws and full-blown ha-ha-has.

The princess, who's reviewin' the scorecards, looks up and is taken aback. She nearly knocks over her chair, and yelps. That's somethin' like gulpin' for air and bitin' a burp at the same time. She ends with a grin and a good-hearted chuckle. That's what she does, and loud enough for all to hear.

"That's one for the money," Jack notes, "if anyone's countin'."

The audience settles down, but keeps up a constant current of conversation with curious comments about Jack and his act. Jack unties the mouse and the palmetto bugs, beggin' a bashful moment from the audience as he relaces and reties his shoe. He explains that this is a safety precaution. He also advises that anyone in the audience with loose footwear, or heavy handbags and the like, might want to lighten the load.

 When he's ready, Jack announces, "Ladies and Gentlemen!" He then claps his hands twice and whistles. The mouse strums and hums. The palmetto bugs hop up to heel 'n' toe and do-si-do.

The audience erupts in laughter. Many people fall out of they seats, some roll in the aisles. The panel of judges laughs as loud as the rest, the princess the loudest of all three. She can't stop herself.

"That's two for the show, don't y'know," says Jack.

The magical mouse music flows over the laughter, and the dancin' palmetto bugs keep busy keepin' everyone in good time a-wigglin' and a-gigglin'. The entire audience is now out they seats a-stampin' they feet. Most high-step like highlanders, some form a conga line, others try to pirouette, a few even dance the Carolina Shag. The two li'l white-haired judges jump atop the table to kick up they heels. But whatever the dance style, Jack has yet to hear the princess laugh over everybody else for a third time. Jack thinks he might strike out, too.

That's when the palmetto bugs start to dance The Chawlstin. They little knees start a-swingin' back 'n' forth 'n' back 'n' forth with a four-arm hand jive, they antennae a-clickin' together in syncopated up and downbeats, they little red 'n' yellow outfits a-blendin' into orange in a speedy smooth slidin' movement. It's a sight never seen before, that's for sure.

The audience is awash in a new wave of laughter. The princess, too, is swept up in the delight of the sight, and she laughs so loud she shakes all over in near delirium. That too, is a sure sight never before seen.

"That's three to go!" claims Jack.

The princess is laughin' so heartily and shakin' so hard, she's about to lose all muscle control and slide underneath the table, but Jack reaches out to catch her. He grabs her, she grabs him, and they tumble together like wrestlers. When they right themselves again, the princess gives Jack a kiss on the cheek. She can't help herself.

"Well, I'll be," says Jack, dumbfounded.

"Only if I can be with you," replies the princess, and winks at Jack.

For a split second Jack doesn't hear the laughter or the music. All he can take in is the pretty smile of the pretty young woman before him. His heart is weightless.

Then he comes to. He looks 'round at the mouse and palmetto bugs, gives a whistle and claps his hands twice. The mouse stops the music, and pants to catch its breath. The dancin' palmetto bugs fall against each other, back to back, and slide to the floor.

The audience freezes in motion. Then suddenly everyone falls down amid such laughter that does the heart good. The three judges make they way back to they seats at the table, and collect the scattered scorecards. The audience finds seats again, and quiets down as the judges tabulate scores and confer on a winner.

In a few minutes, they have decided, and the decision is unanimous. They call all the other contestants to return to the stage in review. Each entertainer is announced again in turn, and the audience applauds wholeheartedly for every one. When Jack is named, the applause becomes raucous, with high-pitched whistles and salutations of praise. Jack is clearly the winner of the "Laff-on Test."

The three judges award Jack the grand prize, and a photographer snaps some pictures for the press. When that's done, Jack carefully collects his crew and sits down for an interview with a local reporter. When they finish, Jack eagerly looks 'round for the princess. She's waitin' in the wings for him.

After that, Jack and the princess, whose name is Mary, get married. She becomes his agent, and in Las Vegas Jack and his act wholly wow the crowds. His mama moves into a penthouse and is ever after as happy as can be. Jack, the hum-strum mouse and the dancin' palmetto bugs are now on tour—maybe you've seen 'em somewhere—and they's rumors of a possible TV show, too. Ain't life funny?

I couldn't say nothing to Jim then. I was laughing too hard.

The Peddler of Golden Dreams

My friend Jim Aisle, renowned as the Lowcountry Liar, is our neighbor-hood storyteller. He is well versed in local history, lives aboard his sloop, the Coota. *There was a time when he was not so sure he had even that for a home—things were desperate for him and he had few options. But like Jim says, "They's more to dreams than just wishin', and they's more to the sea than just fishin'."*

It was what you call the horns of a dilemma. Bein' 'tween a rock and a hard place, with quicksand for real estate in the 'tween space. Well, more like pluff mud, this bein' the Lowcountry and all. My bo-it, the *Coota*, my most valuable possession as well as my humble mobile marine home, was desperately in need of repairs. She needed to be overhauled, put up in dry dock, stripped, caulked, repainted, the works. Besides, they was some interior work I needed to do, some improvements I wanted to make. All the things needin' to be done I had listed and outlined on various work orders with sundry subcontractors. Some of the work got initiated, too, but after goin' through the expense to hoist the *Coota* clean out the water and berth her down to Folly Beach, my bankroll rolled snake eyes.

See, now, I could've used the *Coota* to play tour guide for out-of-towners or to catch enough fish to pay for the overhaul, but the bo-it was already in dry dock, ready to be repaired. Unfortunately, the repairs couldn't be paid for, at least not right at present. And of course, to be on the safe side, the overhaul needed to be done first, in order to go fishin' or play tour guide, which would cover the cost of repairs. But then, that gets me back to the *Coota* sittin' high and dry on Folly. All in a circle it was, and it felt like it was circlin' the drain.

I was in deep pluff mud.

Till now, I had been stayin' aboard the *Coota*, till my funds, as well as my promises to pay, were too low for anyone's interest. Money was short and credit was shorter, so work was at a stand-still; everythin' was pendin' a liberal lubrication of the grease of commerce. Finally, the creditors were kept at bay, satisfied to keep an eye of interest on the *Coota*, by considerin' it as collateral in lieu of payment. We all cosigned an official agreement on the last day of August, with a deadline of six weeks for full payment, or else I lost my bo-it. Most of my gear and all the heavy equipment for my livelihood was secured and battened down.

Thus and so, the particular points to the horns of my dilemma. Now, I only had time on my hands. My worry was I'd lose my home, my livelihood, my main mode of transportation, my mobile lifestyle, everythin'.

While the *Coota* was in dry dock hock, I was livin' out of a duffle bag. I couldn't stay aboard any longer, but I had a buddy, Josh O'Conor, livin' with he family down to Folly Beach, who could put me up for a spell till I squared things. Josh was happily settled with he wife Betty and they three kids, Rusty, Mary Jane, and Christopher. They welcomed me warmly into they home. I was glad to be there—it was a good home base.

On that first night at the O'Conors, the Friday before Labor Day, it just so happened that Josh and some buds from work were employed in the roastin' of a hog for an annual get-together. Josh and he buds worked for the city of Chawl-stin's Streets and Sidewalks Department as a repair crew, so they been always diggin' up relics, even live shells, and had great stories to tell. For the last four years they'd held an annual hog roast hosted by each crew member in turn, and this year Josh had taken the fifth. The road crew had been workin' in shifts since midweek, diggin' a pit mostly, but overall doin' the prep work for the roastin'.

The spot picked for the pit was a hill of sorts—for the Lowcountry—right in Josh's back yard. The story was, the hill was the remains of a Federal bunker or battery, from 'round 1863, '4, '5, when the Yankee army was crawlin' all over Folly. It was solid sand. The bunker hill reminded me of the local legendary half-built fort of sand and palmetto logs on Sullivan's Island, across the harbor, where the Colonial militia defended Chawl-stin from the British in 1776. That victory, over both the army and navy of the supposedly invincible British Empire, convinced the American delegates meetin' up to Philadelphia in late June and early July to "hang together" and cosign the Declaration of Independence. Yessuh, in Chawl-stin, even the sand is historic.

Well, shovelin' in turns, the road crew put a huge hole in the hill. Next, they laid down a bed of charcoal and hickory chips. They set up the frame for the spit, and spitted the hog. Then they brought out the brushes and barbecue sauces to begin the bastin' as the hog roasted. Over the followin' twenty-four hours this endeavor would result in one side of the hog painted with a tomato-based barbecue sauce, givin' it a reddish colorin', while the other side was painted with a mustard-based sauce, givin' the hog a yellow hue.

In teams of three, the road crewmen stood watches over the roastin', all the while fortified with sandwiches, munchies, and beer, under the watchful eye of the master fire tender, Mr. Jack Daniels. So, while I was in the throes of arrangin' the contractual bet on the *Coota*, and movin' onto dry land, these bubbas—an enterprisin', integrated, interestin' group—had been creatin' the makin's of a bona fide shindig. My regret was missin' out on the hog roastin' process—swappin' stories and such, nothin' I hadn't done before—but I would not be denied the bountiful feast prepared.

All afternoon the crewmen had gathered they families and

friends, and everyone brought somethin' to eat or drink. By sun-set we were ready for supper. Along with the hog of two sauces we had red rice, also white rice and field peas, baked beans with bacon, three kinds of macaroni and cheese, a cold macaroni salad, five cole slaws, a coupla veggie trays full of crisp greenery, dozens of hard-boiled eggs dusted with paprika, and enough biscuits and corn bread to fill a Volkswagen van. They was Southern iced tea, sweet as sunshine, and a coupla kegs on tap. We all had a great time, with great food and great friends. It seemed almost a dream, too good to be true.

Whenever I fell asleep, it was on a spare mattress set up in the den—I remember landin' with a *flop!* The mattress was too short and too narrow, definitely not "just right," but I was so tired and wore out and well fed, I just flopped down and snoozed till Saturday mornin'.

Or at least I tried to. In the meantime, in dream time, they came to me a vision, I guess, of a Colonial man, in breeches, waistcoat, and tricornered hat. He pointed at me, then pointed away, to the north. Then he spoke, "Go to Columbia, to the cap-ital. Go to the Gervais Street Bridge, spannin' the Congaree Ribbah. There you will hear what you need to know."

Now, I don't know 'bout readin' dreams, or seein' into the future, so I wasn't sure what to make of the vision. Besides, it was nearly noon before I was willin' to be awake. Took me a little time to focus enough to realize I was awake. Then again, it bein' a Saturday, and with the remains of the roast on hand to dis-mantle, they wasn't much motivation for action.

I put the vision aside as part of the revelry from Friday night, and went about enjoyin' Saturday with Josh and the fine family O'Conor. Betty updated me on Rusty, Mary Jane, and Christopher as we all sat 'round the livin' room. The kids sat through the embarrassment till Betty completed her catalog and took a breath. I just listened, and kept sippin' iced tea. I told some stories then, while various and sundry friends dropped in, till by candle-lightin' time we had warmed up the leftovers, installed another keg, and commenced to repeat the past repast.

That Saturday night, I opted for the couch in the den rather than the little mattress. The couch had wide strips of leather crisscrossin' in a tic-tac-toe design, and my bare skin stuck to the leather like Velcro. The cushions were covered in some scratchy material, and they were lumpy, so I sagged here, bulged there. I tried to sleep, but couldn't get comfortable, till out of sheer exhaustion, I slumbered.

That's not all I did. That same night, the dream or vision or whatever from Friday night reappeared. Definitely, it was a man of the Colonial era, probably from the time of the American Revolution. He had a white cockade on he hat, which I know we Americans wore as a sign of rebellion against the British Empire. Who was this man? The Swamp Fox?

He pointed away and spoke to me again, "Go to Columbia, your state capital. Look at a map. The line between Lexington and Richland Counties is the Congaree Ribbah. Go there, to the Congaree, to the Gervais Street Bridge, to hear what you should hear. Heed what I say."

Come Sunday mornin', I wasn't sure what to think. What was this Colonial man tryin' to relay to me? I wondered if the Colonial man was maybe an ancestor of mine, since my family goes back to pre-Revolution days in the Carolina Colony. Maybe he had come to warn me of some catastrophe. Then again, I was in dire straits already. Yet he would have me travel one hundred miles to the center of South Carolina to listen to a ribbah? What was crazier, this vision or takin' the advice given in the vision?

I was curious about this mystery, and the more I thought about it, the more real it seemed to me. I thought of discussin' the details with Josh, but it bein' a Sunday mornin', the family was fixin' to go to church, so I decided to tag along and worship. I figured I could use any help available, whatever my worry.

After service, I felt more at ease, and put the nocturnal apparition out of my mind. We all relaxed for the rest of the Sabbath; I walked awhile along the seafront, watchin' the breakers roll onto the beach. Later we gathered for supper and they was still plenty of roast hog with the fixin's, so we all pitched in and filled our plates again. In the mornin' the kids would rendezvous back at the church with other campers who were bussin' down to Beaufort for a regional church camp and retreat. Since Rusty, Mary Jane, and Christopher would be gone all week, I told 'em some stories before they went off to bed, and the day ended with a satisfyin' peace.

That night, I pulled a Pawleys Island hammock from the garage, strung it up in the screened porch on the side of the house. Now that was more like it, more like home aboard the *Coota*. A comfortable breeze came slidin' through the screened porch—or piazza, as we say in Chawl-stin—and I swung slightly in the hammock. Finally, I did sleep soundly—for a while.

For the third night in a row, wouldn't y'know it? I had that confounded Continental conjure come to me in my sleep. Whoever he had been, this ghost of some Revolutionary relative of mine, he must have no doubt been a rebel. He was surely turnin' my world upside down.

Once more he pointed at me, then away, and spoke. "Go now, you must not wait. Go to Columbia, to the Congaree Ribbah, to the Gervais Street Bridge. You will hear what you will hear—there! Take a bus, rent a car, hitch a ride, but go to the Gervais Street Bridge. Do it now!"

I woke up. I sat up, nearly fell out the hammock. Focusin' on the darkness, I was tryin' to see if they was anythin' to see. Right then, it finally got through to me: this was a bona fide vision, a dream with a command, a bequest for a quest. I still had some questions about how I would do it, but I was resolved to visit the Gervais Street Bridge. In daylight.

Come day-clean Monday mornin', I told Josh I had some urgent business in Columbia that should take me a day or two to deal with, and I asked to borrow his hammock for the duration. Why, Josh, he was a real buddy. He said sure, and even though he couldn't go with me on such short notice, he offered to pay for my round-trip bus fare. I was so broke I had to say yes. Betty made me some sandwiches—barbecue pork, don't y'know—which I added to my bundle of necessities. I caught the noon bus to Columbia from the Greyhound bus terminal downtown on Society Street, waved goodbye to Josh, and settled in for the ride. It was almost three o'clock that afternoon when I disembarked at the Gervais Street bus stop in Columbia. I grabbed my bundle, hefted the hammock over my shoulder, and marched down to the ribbah. On the west side of Columbia, Gervais Street is a wide boulevard rollin' down a long, slopin' hillside from the capitol grounds to the Congaree.

I stashed my gear in a thick stand of trees among the underbrush along the bank on the Lexington County side. They was a restaurant, *Buddy's By-the-River,* that sat on the high ribbahbank across from a five-point intersection of roadways. One road ran along the ribbah, one ran up a steep hill, another cut straight through a quiet neighborhood of mill houses, still another led west to Lexington County, and I was on the road to and from the bridge. With lots of options to operate with, I figured a popular restaurant was a good base for my informal visit to Columbia.

For the rest of the day I scanned my new neighborhood, gettin' my bearin's. The traffic flashed by, and the few pedestrians who padded by either greeted me with a friendly nod in passin', or else crossed on the other side of the bridge. I never heard a word, let alone *the* word or words, as had been foretold. I figured maybe I needed to give it a full day's wait, so I retired to make a night of it in the hammock strung up in the trees between the ribbah and the restaurant.

As I passed 'round the back of *Buddy's* to get my gear and set up, I saw one of the cook staff on a smoke break, hangin' out on the ribbahside veranda built there. It was a quiet spot. He was a beefy guy, with a stained apron coverin' his girth. The sudden sort of meetin' was unexpected, and we paused.

Then I said, "Howdy, nice night."

The cook, or whatever he was, nodded as he took a drag, exhaled smoke and said, "Sure is. Nice night." The ice sort of broken, I nodded back, and walked on, followin' a trail down the overgrown bank.

The off thing is, that first night, under the stars beside the

Congaree, was the first night without the Continental conjure comin' and commandeerin' my dreams. Could be I was just so dog tired that even the vision went on vacation. I woke up relaxed, refreshed, and ready to take on the quest.

All day Tuesday I paced the length of the Gervais Street Bridge on both sides of the street. All day long—more than twelve hours of walkin' over the ribbah—I watched a parade of cars, cabs and busses, cycles and cyclists, and nearly every type of truck, from pickups to semis. I tried to be nonchalant with pedestrians, 'specially after I'd race across on-comin' traffic to greet 'em. And still, from the random sample of the thirty-seven passersby that day, not a single one of 'em had more than the time of day to tell me.

In the afternoon, about a quarter to four, I noted the cook again out back of *Buddy's* on a smoke break. He saw me, too; I nodded, waved, he raised a hand. He seemed a friendly enough fellow—a hard worker workin' hard.

When I packed it in for the day, 'round nine o'clock that night, I had eaten the last of Betty's barbecue sandwiches, so I thought to check a menu at *Buddy's*. I figured I might have enough scratch for a few days' fare if need be, though I hoped it need not be. I got a coffee and a slice of hot apple pie. It was good to get off of my feet, sittin' in the booth, feelin' like a customer.

After I finished eatin', it was time to turn in, so I paid the bill, left a tip—I cannot not help out, no matter my matters, y'know? As I was walkin' 'round the back again I met the cook there on the little veranda, again on break, eatin' from a plate, mindin' he own quiet business.

Again we nodded, looked eye to eye. He was busy chewin', so I said, "Nice night tonight, too." He swallowed, smiled, and said, "Yeah, it is. Nice night, yeah." I tipped my hat to him and passed on to my gear in the woods.

That night, that second night in the hammock by the Congaree, my Continental cousin's vision revisited me. This night he didn't seem threatenin' or demandin', though, but rather reassurin', I guess. He been busy devourin' a chicken leg, which is somethin' I hadn't realized been a common practice for ghosts or visions. He mumbled between bites—that leg looked good, too—somethin' like, "Soon, soon. So far, so good. Soon you will know what you need to hear. Soon." Then he licked his lips and faded till he disappeared.

I awoke Wednesday kinda groggy, and later in the mornin' than I meant to. I was hungry, too, with a strong hankerin' for bacon and eggs. I went back to *Buddy's* and splurged for that, along with grits, toast, OJ, and three cups of coffee. So fortified for the day, I hiked back up to the bridge to continue the vigil for my vision.

It was another day paced away. No one who walked past—and only a coupla dozen folks did—spoke of anythin' I thought remarkable. For long spells of waitin' I leaned over the bridge, watchin' the ribbah rush by. A coupla fishermen waded into the water about fifty yards downstream, and I waved to 'em, but they never looked up long enough to notice. They were fishin', after all, and fishin' is all about patience and endeavor. The focus is on the fish. Guess I was kinda fishin', too.

While I was contemplatin' the current and my current events, out popped the cook on the veranda below for he quarter-to-four smoke break. He lit up and saw me some twenty feet above him on the bridge, and he stopped, blinked, smoke liftin' from the cigarette in he mouth and the match in his hand. I waved, smiled, and said, "Hey! How ya doin'?"

"Whatcha doin'?" he asked. "You been here all week hangin' 'round. You know I've seen you. Whatup with that?"

What could I tell him that I truly believed myself? I grinned thinkin' about it all, while the cook literally fumed. I said, "Well-suh, you may not believe me to tell it, but I was havin' trouble sleepin' the last few nights. Kept havin' this vision, a visitor, who kept tellin' me to come to this bridge."

"You don't say!" the cook interrupted me. "What a coincidence! As a matter of fact, I've been havin' a dream for the last three nights in a row. I see some soldier, a Minute Man, I think,

The Peddler of Golden Dreams   **105**

and he's marchin' along, with a shovel instead of a rifle, or a mus-
ket, I guess. He's mutterin' somethin' too, only I can't hear him
till he stops at a little hill. He's sayin', *'Folly, folly, this is all folly.
Folly.'* I tell ya, buddy, it all seemed like folly to me. Dreams is
such foolishness sometimes."

The cook looked at his watch, took a drag, and turned to the
back door. I thought he might suddenly leave. I called out, "Was
they more to the soldier—I mean, your dream, your story?"

The cook took another drag, exhaled, and said back, "Well,
yeah, sure was. This soldier, he's at this little hill, but it's kinda
tropical, with palm trees and all 'round. And he's diggin' into the
hill, from the top, like he's diggin' a grave, and he's all the time
mutterin', *'Folly, this is folly.'* But he's not diggin' a grave, I guess,
'cause when the hole's deep enough, the soldier goes off, then
comes back pullin' and tuggin' a big old-timey chest. It's big as
one of our freezer chests inside, only not all chrome, but wood
and brass and all."

The cook paused, pulled on his cigarette. "You sure you
wanna hear the rest of my dream?" he asked me, like he was
wastin' my time. "I mean, it's all so weird, silly."

"Sure," I told him. I told myself I wouldn't miss it for the
world, I told myself. This is why I came here, I'm sure. "Go on,"
I said.

Chucklin', the cook shook his head. "Okay," he said. "Well,
this Minute Man has dug this hole in the hill, right? He drags
over a huge ol' chest. Now he maneuvers it into the hole. He
shoves and pushes and tugs and pulls; it's like watchin' a fisher-
man fightin' a catch, and he finally lands the chest square in the
hole. It goes *plop!* And the lid pops open, springs back, like on
cue, y'know? And inside, get this, inside the chest ain't no gold,
no treasure, just a big geen sea turtle! Can you believe that? A
turtle! A big, pea-soup-green sea turtle! Then, he winks, I swear,
he winks at me in my sleep"

I had to interrupt, and asked him, "Who winked at you? The
soldier, or the turtle?"

The cook winced and said, "The turtle, man, the turtle! I told ya it was silly. And then, that's it. End of dream. End of story. Now, can you believe any of that, mister?"

Cookie went on smokin', while I took it all in, what he had said of his dream. I had some homework to do now. I accumulated it all as best as I could connect it. They was the Continental soldier, maybe an ancestor of mine, an enterprisin' sort, with a shovel, diggin' a hole in a little bunker, a hill, so he could bury a chest holdin' a flirtatious sea turtle. That was some dream, which is what I told the cook.

"Yeah," he said. Then he looked again at he watch, stubbed out he smoke, and said, "Hey, gotta go. See ya. Nice talkin' to ya." He waved and went back into *Buddy's*, and I waved back, my hand just swingin' back and forth as I did the math.

Standin' there mullin' over the information, I realized the little bunker, that hill he spoke of with the palm trees, sounded a lot like Josh's backyard. Right where the road crew dug the pit for the hog roast. Could they be some treasure there, buried beneath the pit? And that turtle, that was a clue, no doubt. Must be the *Coota*.

By now I figured I had heard exactly whatever it was I supposedly was sent to hear on the Gervais Street Bridge over the Congaree Ribbah in the state capital of Columbia. My work here was done. I was satisfied, though I knew this still wasn't the end of the quest. I had to return to Chawl-stin, to Folly Beach, to Josh's backyard. I had to find that chest.

First things first, I was hungry. So, one last time I sat down to dine at *Buddy's*. I ordered a chef's salad in honor of my new friend, the smokin' cook. When I cleared out, I looked 'round for him, but didn't see him, the will-o'-the-wisp.

I hiked up long, hilly Gervais Street into downtown Columbia, to the Greyhound bus terminal, and caught the last bus to Chawl-stin just before eight o'clock. Durin' the ride homeward, I tried to sleep, but felt too cramped in the seat to even nap. Just as well, since I wasn't sure I wanted any visionary visitors.

'Round 'bout eleven-thirty Wednesday night, I was wearily

gatherin' my gear at the downtown Chawl-stin Greyhound bus depot on Society Street. About fifteen minutes later, I caught the last bus to Folly at King and Wentworth, and so, by the stroke of midnight, I passed over the Ashley Ribbah Bridge. Another body of movin' water. Seemed sort of an ironic acknowledgement of my adventure, a mystical transition with magical transportation, and maybe treasure.

I disembarked at last, in front of the little Folly Beach Library about a quarter past one, Thursday mornin'. I hoisted the hammock like a yoke over my shoulders, and walked for nearly an hour before arrivin' at long last where Josh had cut out the letters for "O'Conor" displayed at the front of he house on a shingle.

The house was still, everyone quietly asleep. I unbundled my bundle, slung up the hammock in the piazza, and crawled in to finally rest. Y'know, I couldn't. Maybe it was from bein' wound up from the road trip, or the unrest in the bus seat. No doubt, my deep thoughts were on that chest of possible treasure. As I lay in the hammock tryin' not to bring it to the surface of concern, an owl hooted nearby, repeatedly. My eyes blinked open, but all I could focus on was across the yard, bathed in a serene stream of moonlight. It was Hog Roast Hill.

The owl hooted again, and I wondered if my ghostly cousin in the vision had a vengeful streak in him. I said aloud, "No more." I tried to sleep again, determined to sort things out in the sunshine.

The owl hoot-hooted some more. What an alarm clock. They was no sense in sleepin'. I was in the midst of forces unseen, but apparently, all-seein'. What else could I do?

I climbed out of the hammock, and in the unfoldin' to stand up, my joints played paradiddles of *snap! crackle! pop!* Nothin' like the expectation of hard labor to get the kinks out, and maybe tire me enough to really sleep.

I grabbed my flashlight and found a shovel in the garage. At the hog pit I just stood starin' down into the dark remains for a few minutes. The night was cool for early September, with a gusty wind, but the air was wet, as usual, 'specially on the island.

The darkness became a deeper dark with a gray fog that slipped over everythin', makin' things clear as mud.

I began diggin'. At first tentatively, gingerly, but eventually furiously flingin' the dirt out. After a solid hour o' diggin', I was knee-deep into the pit. I took a short break to catch a breath and to watch the night sky. The wet foggy air was too dark to discern shapes, but somehow, somewhere way up there, through the soggy haze, I could see a twinkle or two.

I went back to work. The wind would whip up every so often and sand sometimes stung me. I worried my diggin' would awaken Josh, the family, and the neighbors, but the hill and the house were spaced well enough apart to avoid detection. Besides, the gusty wind rose up loud enough, and it bein' so dark and murky, nobody coulda seen what was goin' on. I began widenin' the hole all 'round by 'bout another foot, and by five in the mornin' I was in over my head, a measurable stoppin' point.

I wasn't sure I could continue. Slumped against the wall of the earth I had just excavated, my body told me I needed sleep as much as stamina. I was all for callin' it a night, callin' it quits, when that owl hooted again, and the wind suddenly kicked up.

I was too scared to close my eyes. I was too tired to run from any haint that happened by. I was too deep in the hole, quite literally, to do anythin' other than watch and wait to see what happened.

The wind whipped back and forth, whistlin', roarin', offerin' up arias with ghostly gusts of night air. Before I could decide to climb out the hole and go climb back into the hammock, he appeared. My dream vision Continental soldier was a-peerin' over the other side of the pit. He said nothin', only pointed, and stared with wide eyes.

Slowly, I positioned the flashlight, picked up the shovel, and aimin' approximate to where he directed, I proceeded to shovel up some fine Folly real estate. Then they was a *thunk!* I couldn't believe I heard it at first.

Thunk! Thunk! They was somethin' there. I fumbled for my flashlight, threw the beam over the bottom of the pit, and there, clearly, was the top of a chest. The wood hadn't splintered when I hit it. Good, the chest was intact, so I dug and scraped till I had outlined the lid. It measured about a yard, likely a meter, length times width. I had no idea how deep it really was.

I turned to look up at the soldier. He stood still, arms crossed, head a-noddin', with a big grin. Then he took off he tricornered hat, and saluted me with a stiff bow. He may have been wipin' away ghostly tears, but in the predawn darkness it was difficult to know.

Then this ghost did another odd thing, or so it seemed. Must be a different code of conduct for the ephemeral ones. He popped off one of the brass buttons on he coat and looked at it before tossin' it down to me. I reached down for the button, tried to pick it out of the dirt, but saw nothin', and then looked up to see—nothin'. Nobody. No vision, no ghost, just the very first hint of sunrise slippin' over the horizon.

I had to hide the chest, the hole, my work. I fetched a blue tarp from my gear, and placed it over the hole, pegged it down with large seashells the kids had collected into a pile in the backyard. Josh would be up soon, gettin' ready, and goin' to work. I needed rest. It may be backwards goin' to bed at daybreak, but lately I'd been keepin' regular nocturnal company. Anyway, Josh and the family wouldn't mind me hangin' out, hangin' 'round, y'know. I climbed back into the hammock, and last remember hearin' Betty callin' Josh to get up, before I thankfully fell asleep.

Not long after noon, Thursday, I heard birds chirpin', singin', carryin' on, raisin' a ruckus, and I woke up. A fat tabby cat was creepin' across the backyard, headin' for the blue tarp and the hole. If that feline had any basal thought for a moment to facilitate hisself of my hard work for he own sand box, he was about to have eight more lives to figure it out.

I rolled out, landed lightly on my feet like, well, like a cat. I had seen a slingshot and pellets somewhere 'round here, but before I could locate 'em, that cat came to the corner of the blue tarp. I had to settle for a loud handclap to scare off the cat—it jerked at first shock, then shot off, jumped a fence, and was gone.

I ventured outside, 'round the house, Josh's truck and Betty's van were gone. I went inside, found a note they wrote, waitin' for me on the kitchen table. The note read:

> *Hey Jim—Josh is at work and I have some shopping and chores to do. Josh and I have a league game up at Folly Alleys, so we'll eat there. Be home between 10 and 11.*
>
> *—Betty*
>
> *P.S. Make yourself at home.*

Added below, in Josh's handwritin', was:
> *J—Saw the tarp. Thanks for covering the hog pit. Might be dangerous.—J*

Well, shoot, with everyone out the house till ten tonight, I had eight, nine hours to dig up the chest. First, I took a shower, a long-time-no-see friend, and it was marvelous to get reacquainted. Afterwards, I created sort of a sub sandwich from fixin's in the fridge; I'd had my fill of barbecue pork for a spell. I pulled out one of the three plastic gallon jugs of iced tea from the fridge, too, took it to refresh me while I worked.

By quarter to two I was diggin' again, hungry to see the contents of the chest. By two-thirty the entire perimeter 'round the lid was exposed, with clearance to swing open fully on the hinge. By the time three o'clock was approachin', I had uncovered the front hasp, and a massive brass padlock clamped through it. I fetched a crowbar from Josh's garage, and worked against that lock, pushin', pryin', then *bam!* It broke.

I had to catch my breath. It was Lowcountry hot and muggy, and I was diggin' my own grave, if I wasn't careful, but I was also anticipatin' the liftin' of the lid. I took off the padlock—must have weighed five, six pounds, a clunky thing—set it aside at the top of the hole. Then I brushed off my hands, took a breath, undid the hasp, lifted the lid.

At first, the sunshine caught the glint, and it blinded me like a flash bulb surprise when I threw back the lid to introduce to the world the chest full of gold coins. British, they were, stamped with a profile and the name of HRH King George III of Great Britain. They was documentation too, preserved in an old oilskin packet. I scanned the quill-and-ink writin', takin' in the who, what, and when.

This was service pay meant to be meted out by a quartermaster, under His Royal Majesty's etcetera, etcetera. This was a special chest of specie, as they called it, to pay not the British soldiers, nor to bribe Patriots to turn coat, but to satisfy a basic lust for profit, 'specially at the expense of others. A *schadenfreude* fortune. This be a chest of what is known as Hessian gold, payable— and specifically so stated—to the German mercenary troops accompanyin' the British forces. Royal blood money for those that money could buy; and besides, ol' George III was a Hanover King, more *ein Deutscher* than *Englischer*.

I don't know how much time passed as I stared at, then inspected, my find, but finally I closed the lid and began diggin' 'round the chest again. The repeated motions of stabbin' into the dirt, liftin' a blade-full, tossin' it out the hill, allowed me room for thinkin' of my options, and how to achieve 'em. First of all, of course, was gettin' the chest dug out of the hole.

Hour after hour that hot afternoon I displaced dirt, shovel by shovel, leavin' about a foot of space all 'round the chest. I continued diggin' another six inches or so, to the front and back of the chest, and then I excavated a narrow tunnel beneath it. I had noticed earlier the rear-mounted winch on Josh's work truck, figured I'd loop the chest and pull it out the hole with the cable. I finished the dig by cuttin' out a wedge of earth that left a rudimentary ramp at the rear of the hole. They was room enough to back up the work truck, loop the chest with the winch cable, and pull it to the surface.

I had dug on, as the sun set, with the sky slowly turnin' into colors of cool blues and a rich rainbow of yellows to orange to pink to magenta, till indigo enveloped everythin', and the light of day was done. So far, so good. I wrapped the chest with the blue tarp, tied it 'round, and covered the hole with some panels of plywood Josh had stacked against the back of the garage. All the documents and a dozen of the coins I stashed in my duffle bag, for ease of reference. The proof positive to this mystery would be in how these coins wound up on Folly Beach, under Josh's backyard barbecue pit, and that may tell me why I had to find 'em. I was eager to prove the provenance of the coins, as well as to identify and verify my spectral ancestor. I just had to uncover the context to the clues that made up this particular *e pluribus unum*.

Just after nine-thirty, I was washed, dried, pressed, and dressed when the phone rang. It was Betty, askin' me if I wanted a burger, since she and Josh were gonna stop on the way home. I said, sure, thanks, no onions. I didn't want indigestion and bad dreams.

While we filled up on the burgers and fries, Betty filled me in on the activities of the day, the kids, her world. When she took a bite, I asked Josh for a ride into town in the mornin' and he nodded, swallowed, said, "Yeah, sure, gotta leave by eight. Drop you off where?"

"Library," I said. "Downtown, King Street."

"Marion Square?" Josh said, "Not a problem."

That night I musta gone straight to deep sleep, I was so wore down and wore out. All I remember was crawlin' into the hammock, and wakin' up when it was Friday mornin'. Josh was standin' next to me with two cups of steamin' coffee in he hands, sayin', "Yo, Jimbo! Time to git up and go!"

On the ride into Chawl-stin, I innocently queried Josh about the horsepower, torque, and maneuverability of the work truck, and how he used the winch. He proudly told me the specs, and some stories 'bout usin' the winch. He dropped me off at the library, I told him I'd be here at six, at closin', and we parted.

Inside, at the reference desk, I met some nice librarians who helped me research the coins, which I had bagged up and brought with me. The librarians *oohed* and *aahed* at the pristine quality of the coins, in awe of the vintage of the mintage. They also tracked down data on my genealogy, and relevant facts of the

Revolution in and 'round Chawl-stin harbor. I left 'em to answer those questions, and to index some legal points about state, federal, and international ownership. From a list prepared by the same friendly librarians, I started out to visit some coin experts and antiques assessors for confirmation and confidentiality of my find—on the promise of a generous commission, of course.

All day long I went to offices, displayed the coins, presented the quill-and-ink papers, and vaguely explained my backstory. I was met with considerable respect by all the reviewers. I collected reports, a coupla catalogs on coinage, and lots of business cards. One expert very calmly said, "Sir, if this is the only sample you have, it is worth a small fortune. If you possess more," and here he inhaled deeply, "you may be wealthy beyond your dreams."

It was late in the afternoon, close to closin', when I got back to the library. The librarians had waitin' for me a folder with printouts and photocopies coverin' everythin' I had asked about—a wealth of information. I even learned a new word for coin expertise: numismatics. I always say, every day is worth learnin' somethin' new. Anyway, I was so grateful for all they hard work, I took down the names of those good Samaritan librarians for future reference.

I was readin' over some of the papers outside the library, when Josh arrived to pick me up. On the ride home he talked about a party over to the Isle of Palms that he and Betty were goin' to later, and he reminded me that the kids were at camp till next weekend. That was fine with me I told him, I had some readin' to do.

Josh and Betty left about eight-thirty, takin' the van. The keys to the work truck were among Josh's stuff on he dresser in the bedroom, which I discovered durin' a quick reconnoiter of the house. In no time, I had the truck reversed and parked by the hole.

I pulled away the plywood panels and laid 'em like a wooden carpet along the cut-away earthen ramp. I ran the winch cable down, under, and 'round and 'round the chest, makin' sure the tension would hold. Then, with a short prayer repeated under my breath, I revved the engine, began windin' up the winch, and the treasure tug-o'-war began.

At first nothin' budged. Then the cable *twanged*, and they was a stretched out suckin' sound, then a *kuh-whup!* and a *thump!* I felt that. Yessuh, it was a gen-u-wine somethin' goin' *bump* in the night. Slowly, slowly, the chest rose up off its centuries-old restin' place, and was pulled out of the hole along the boarded ramp to the surface, till it rested on a coupla two-by-fours on the ground.

For the next coupla hours I worked that chest across Josh's backyard, usin' the winch and the truck, makin' paths of plywood panelin' to slide the treasure over the lawn. I positioned the chest, still roped and wrapped in my blue tarp, against the back of the garage, and surrounded it with restacked plywood. I was policin' up the yard, when I heard the phone ringin' again, and again it was Betty.

She told me that Josh was "a little tipsy" for automotive safety, and she didn't want to make the drive home either, so they were gonna spend the night out at the beach house on the Isle of Palms with they hosts. I told her to beware; they may get stuck on the IOP, the Isle of (Perpetual) Parties. She laughed. I told her everythin' was fine with me, fine with the house, fine with whatever they wanted to do. I figured it just gave me more time to finish up my work.

It was already Saturday, but I went back out into the night, shovel in hand, to fill in the hole. This was so much easier and faster than diggin' out; sort of like when you take a trip and it always seems to take longer gettin' there than gettin' back. Spade by spade, I shoveled the dirt back into the huge hole I had made. It was goin' for three in the mornin', when I decided I had thrown in enough dirt to un-hole the hill.

I was too tired to dream again, leastways I don't recall any more visions with a mission. I figured if I were to see my ancestor's spectre, he'd appear when he was ready. No use lookin' for trouble, intangible as it may seem.

I woke at midmornin', stumbled 'round the kitchen, breakin' eggs and breakin' in the day. By my third cup of coffee I had breakfast removed, got out the research paperwork, and began readin' the details. They was some devilish details, too.

Here's what I found out from the librarians researchin' on the sundry subjects I suggested. The long-lost so-called Hessian gold was indeed the service pay for the German mercenaries, who arrived here on they initial Southern excursion in June 1776 aboard British battleships with Generals Clinton and Cornwallis. At the time, our American defensive line was behind a half-built fort of sand and palmetto logs hastily thrown together on Sullivan's Island, but our determination to fight and to win was as strong as stone.

Durin' this first major attempt by the Royal British Army and Navy to capture Chawl-stin—"the jewel of the South"— the Hessians didn't get a chance to fight; as it happened, they never even disembarked. That was lucky. Cornwallis and his troops got stuck and nearly stranded on what is now the Isle of Palms, while the commodore of the fleet, Sir Peter Parker, literally had his pants shot off him.

The fleet had to flee, but the pilots weren't sure of the shoals and sandbars even at high tide, and besides, the wind was calm. All the while the battle raged on. One of they ships, the *Actaeon*, ran aground in the middle of the channel, about where Fort Sumter was later built—that's some spot to be in, anytime. The situation was hopeless; the *Actaeon* had to be abandoned, so the Brits fired it up and rowed away. A few fearless, or crazy, Carolinians aboard they ship, the *Prosper,* raced over to salvage many useful items before it all became a lost cause.

So, in order to lighten the load and float out of Chawl-stin harbor to the relative safety of the open sea, His Majesty's sailors jettisoned any dead weight they could lay they hands on. Some of the ballast they tossed overboard straightaway as jetsam, but the more valued cargo, like extra ordnance, soldiers' tents, and officers' livery, were placed in small bo-its that ran trail lines to the ships. The excess weight was off, without the loss of supplies, and it worked—mostly.

You see, in the confusion of the British withdrawal, some-how the chest of Hessian gold was placed in one of the trailin' bo-its, and subsequently, perhaps in part due to the weight of the wealth, the rope broke, and the valuable cargo drifted out to sea on a strong current, last seen roundin' Morris Island towards the Atlantic Ocean. They been too much lead flyin' right then to be overly concerned about unknown gold, so it became merely lost spoils of war. Some historians—cited by the librarians—have speculated that the Hessian gold wound up on Folly Beach somewhere, concealed by the sands of time. Who's to say?

From my pedigree papers the librarians found the record of one James Tomas Aisle, circa 1780. His place of residence was listed as Coffin Island, which was the original name for what is now the island of Folly. My family came over with the great wave of Huguenot immigration long before the Revolution. They carried with 'em what little they had, sort of like my present condition. They had to really earn whatever advantage they could in this new world, and they may not have always been within the limit or the letter of the law. A case in point, for he allegedly questionable activities in and 'round Chawl-stin con-cernin' contraband and smugglin', James, my namesake, was hanged by the British. Maybe he knew somethin' 'bout they chest of missin' mercenary money, like where it was buried. Sounds like ol' Coffin Island James was an entrepreneurial type, always lookin' for an opportunity. Maybe opportunity knocked him down and out. Now opportunity was knockin' again.

So for over two hundred years this gold sat under the sand, and only my executed ancestor knew where. By the time I had come 'round, and bein' in my present situation, now it was time to cash in, I guess, accordin' to my own ghost of the coast. Havin' the same name and bloodline, I suppose, makes for a match between this world we know, and the unknown, unseen world of spirits. Some kind of communication not possibly regulated by the FCC; it's as much feelin' as it is fact.

As far as I could see, or read, they was no one knowin' about this lost gold, no one ever looked for it. Of course, I wasn't lookin' for it either, but I was directed to its location. Now I had to plot a course to keep the treasure, and do with it as I saw fit.

'Round noon, Josh and Betty returned, somewhat sheepish. I didn't say nothin'. The rest of the day we all rested and recuperated. I read and reread all the documents and copies, till I could recite chapter and verse. Josh and Betty felt a little off balance without the kids runnin' 'round, but I believe they enjoyed the calm quiet.

Sunday mornin' we again attended service, myself as much for any forgiveness as for guidance. The kids would be returnin' from camp later in the afternoon, and that was all the agenda for the day. Tomorrow, Rusty, Mary Jane, and Christopher would return to school and life would go on.

That was the plan. Everyone havin' a purpose, and purposely pursuin' it. But, after a week and a half of school, the calendar was thrown out. Everythin' changed in the Lowcountry. Heck, everythin' changed across Carolina.

Hurricane Hugo hit the Lowcountry at the stroke of midnight three weeks into September. It was a day of wind, rain, wind, waves risin', wind, night into day, a long, long day of wind and water, and more wind. Then came the quiet of the eye. And then the wind, all over again. The destruction was tremendous, entire communities reduced to mere campsites. The aftermath for weeks was chaotic. It been a strange time in ol' Chawl-stin, when FEMA became a household word, and nobody meant "thigh bone," neither. They was no anarchy, though the National Guard kept martial law along the shops and stores of King Street. No, actually, everyone became a neighbor, and in no way was it Socialism, but it surely was sociable. Folks have always been neighborly down here.

More to my concern, the unburied treasure had weathered the storm, wrapped snugly in my tarp, though unprotected by the plywood I had stacked 'round it—we boarded up the windows when we battened down the hatches. The weight of the gold was greater than the blow of Hugo, though, unless perhaps ol' Coffin Island James had lent a hand, and somehow secured the treasure chest with an anchor, come high wind or high water. Well-suh, if this wealth was meant to be an heirloom, I was loomin' large to be the heir.

By the time things were right-sided again, I lay claim to the treasure as true salvage, with no other claimants, a verified find. Sundry insurance companies, museum experts, professional numismatists, historians of various studies and countries, as well as the Chawl-stin County Office of Mesne Conveyance, all agreed on the authenticity, value, and ownership. I was heartily gratified. Suddenly I had become an independently wealthy individual. Yet I still had me no more demands than a good breeze to catch a sail, livin' on this coast.

So, after all the dreamin', all my travels and travails, my toil in the soil, my various investigations, my peculiar puzzle been pieced together. After all my expenses, I wound up with ten million dollars. So jus' like a lazy jack, I never again have to work a day in my life for anyone. The *Coota* been shipshape, refitted, better than new. All my debts and creditors been paid up, squared away, and not to forget, the IRS was safely satisfied. My good friends, the family O'Conor, would be well tended for life. The road crews of Chawl-stin's Streets and Sidewalks Department received an anonymous and generous annual donation for a hog roast for as long as they wanted. My pleasant surprise was the purely gracious gratitude of the British experts and officials, the acclimation of the find, which came with a royal award of recognition. I have a ribbon and a little medal in bronze and some certificates statin' my "foresight into the value of the past" as they put it. I suppose.

It's strange, sometimes, what you'll find in life, whether or not you're lookin' for it.

I told Jim, "Heads or tails, you always come up shining with your stories."

"You can bank on it," he told me.

Background Notes

The Legend of the Lowcountry Liar, the story from which this collection gets its title, is the so-called backstory that underlies Jim Aisle's renown. The original is one of my favorite Irish fairy tales, of which there are many variants, in Ireland and the world over.

The Bad Business of Brave Bob is a legendary Lowcountry ghost story and a jump tale to boot. A jump tale has to be heard for effect—the storyteller leads the listener along a tale calmly and confidently, until the climax, and then *Boo! Gotcha!* Audience members "jump" in reaction to the scary punch line. Mark Twain's favorite jump tale was *The Golden Arm*. Like *Brave Bob* it is always a delight for the audience. It is equally fun to tell.

A Lowcountry Whale of a Tale is a survival story generally found among the indigenous peoples of the Pacific Northwest coast culture. In this version I've sampled the local marine life.

Lazy Lucky Lowcountry Jack is my variant of a famous folktale with a pedigree as old as the hills—and here in the Lowcountry, that is saying something. Our local lump of a hill is located east of the Cooper River in the Old Village of Mount Pleasant. Not that it is much of a mount(ain)—a few more horrendous hurricanes like Hugo could easily make it beachfront property. I have added a storyteller's *pourquoi* (storyteller's term from the French word for *why*) at the end to explain the "real" etymology of my family's Florida hometown.

Cold as the Grave is a sad true-love ghost story involving old coastal Carolina clans. This tale is a classic for Halloween night, and is even haunting in broad daylight.

Mr. & Mrs. Vinaigrette is a noodle head story if ever there was one. A noodle head story underscores the loony logic of humanity, with the inevitable mishaps serving as cautionary lessons. Aesop used animals to teach us morality; noodle head stories do that, but they'll make you laugh, too. I have often told a version of this tale called *The Sweet Life of Mr. and Mrs. Vinegar* using shadow puppets. The original is a folktale from the British Isles, with references to the North Britons (Scots). We often mock what we fear (which is why the English try to belittle the Scots), yet despite our fears, we carry on. After all the silliness, this is a tale of perseverance in spite of luck, pluck, or muck.

The Wreck-Construction of the Ashley Ribbah Bridge is a trickster tale that shames the Devil, and is based upon (mostly European) variants concerning bridges. I commissioned this story to coincide with this year's annual Cooper River Bridge Run held here in Charleston.

Reflections on Relations is a story with cousin variants around the globe, wherever there are noodle heads. Maybe someday somewhere there will be a family reunion. Who knows what that assemblage would resemble?

The Luck of the Irish Fella is a hard-luck folk tale with a sweet twist at its happily-ever-after ending. It is too ironic not to have the luck of the Irish in it.

Deep in the Heart of It is a sure-shot example that a bona fide cowboy can spot prime bull from a bum steer.

Dixie's Lowcountry Roots is my own trickster tale with an innocuous haint included in the mix. The ingredients and paraphernalia are from regional recipes for root medicine. Some of it will cure what ails you, and some of it will do the opposite.

Jack and the Dancin' Palmetto Bugs is an old Irish wonder tale originally called *The Bee, the Harp, the Mouse and the Bum-Clock* credited to the late, great *seanchaí* (Irish Gaelic for *storyteller*), Seumas MacManus. A bum-clock is a cockroach (or palmetto bug in the South), because these creepy crawlers dash under furniture such as a big grandfather clock, seeking dark hiding places when the lights come on. The folk instrument played by the mouse is a

Jew's/Jaws/Juice Harp or, as I call the one I play, a *Lowcountry Lyre*.

The Peddler of Golden Dreams is loosely based upon an old folk-tale from the British Isles called *The Peddler of Swatham* (and other variants). In general, a peddler is an itinerant salesman of household goods. In the case of Jim Aisle, who travels the Lowcountry telling his stories, whether you "buy" what he tells you or not is up to you.

Guide to Lowcountry Lingo

Banjaxed Refers to something that is broken, perhaps in pieces, beyond repair; you'll have to rebuild from scratch

Beaufort In South Carolina, this is pronounced like *beautiful*: *Beyoofurt*. Not to be confused with Beaufort *(Bo-fort)*, North Carolina

Bo-it Boat

Boo-hag This hellacious spirit will visit you in the dead of night, sit on your chest as you sleep, and bend down as if to kiss you good night, but instead suck out your ever-loving soul.

Chawl-stin Charleston, South Carolina

Chawls-tonians Residents of the city of Chawl-stin

Chere Here

Conjure A spook, a ghost, or a hag; something that goes *bump!* in the night

Coota (Cooter) 1. A turtle. Turtles are age-old tricksters and very wise. 2. The *Coota* is Jim's sloop—a single-mast, sixty-foot vessel very suitable for the Carolina coast.

Cuppah Ribbah Cooper River

Day-clean Daybreak, sunrise

E pluribus unum A Latin phrase that translates to *out of the many, one*. It is etched onto every American coin. Check the change in your pocket.

Frenstance For instance

Gervais (Street Bridge) Pronounced *Jer-vay*

Great googly-moogly! Lowcountry expression of disbelief; used when "gosh" or "golly" or "wow" just isn't enough

Haint A haunt, spirit, ghost of the Lowcountry

Hanover King A ruler who was of the Hanover (German) lineage of English royalty

Hessian gold Hesse is a large state in Germany. This is a slightly derisive term for the royal English money paid to the professional German soldiers fighting for King George III. The American rebels considered them cutthroat mercenaries.

'Low Allow

Pawleys Island hammock These hand-woven hammocks are the best of the swinging rope beds.

Piazza *(pee-ahhh-za)* The front porch

Porcher Pronounced *por-shay*

Receipt Recipe

Ribbah River

Well-suh Well, sir

Woik Work

Yessuh Yes, sir

If you enjoyed reading this book, here are some other books from Pineapple Press on related topics. For a complete catalog, write to Pineapple Press, P.O. Box 3889, Sarasota, FL 34230 or call 1-800-PINEAPL (746-3275). Or visit our website at www.pineapplepress.com.

Best Ghost Tales of North Carolina and *Best Ghost Tales of South Carolina.* The actors of Carolina's past linger among the living in these thrilling collection of ghost tales. Experience the chilling encounters told by the winners of the North Carolina "Ghost Watch" contest. Use Zepke's tips to conduct your own ghost hunt. (pb)

Coastal North Carolina. Terrance Zepke visits the Outer Banks and the Upper and Lower Coasts to bring you the history and heritage of coastal communities, main sites and attractions, sports and outdoor activities, lore and traditions, and even fun ways to test your knowledge of this unique region. Over 50 photos. (pb)

Coastal South Carolina. Terrance Zepke shows readers historic sites, pieces of history, recreational activities, and traditions of the South Carolina coast. Includes recent and historical photos. (pb)

Legends of the Seminoles by Betty Mae Jumper. This collection of rich spoken tales—written down for the first time—impart valuable lessons about living in harmony with nature and about why the world is the way it is. Each story is illustrated with an original painting by Guy LaBree. (hb, pb)

Sandspun collected by Annette Bruce and J. Stephen Brooks. A collection of tales rich with homespun humor, charm, and wisdom, all told with flair by some of Florida's best storytellers. You'll find ghost stories, tall tales, nature stories, morality tales, and stories that will have you in stitches! Great for reading aloud to children and adults alike. (hb, pb)

Tellable Cracker Tales and *More Tellable Cracker Tales* collected by Annette Bruce. Memorable characters from Florida history come alive in these folktales and legends, tall tales, and gator tales. Pull up your favorite chair and a few listeners and start your own storytelling tradition with the gems in this collection. (hb, pb)

Notes

Notes